The Nightwalker

Belinda Hurmence

The Nightwalker

CLARION BOOKS

TICKNOR & FIELDS: A HOUGHTON MIFFLIN COMPANY

NEW YORK

Clarion Books
Ticknor & Fields, a Houghton Mifflin Company
Text copyright © 1988 by Belinda Hurmence
Frontispiece copyright © 1988 by Alix Berenzy

Library of Congress Cataloging-in-Publication Data
Hurmence, Belinda.
     The nightwalker.
     Summary: Twelve-year-old Savannah wonders if her
little brother Poco, who sleepwalks, is setting the
mysterious fires that are leveling the fishermen's
shacks on the Shackleford Bank near their island home off
the North Carolina coast.
     [1. Arson—Fiction. 2. Sleepwalking—Fiction.
3. Brothers and sisters—Fiction. 4. Islands—Fiction]
I. Title.
PZ7.H9457Ni 1988   [Fic]   88-2827
ISBN 0-89919-732-9

For my sister,
Faun Watson Metcalf

Contents

The Nightwalker

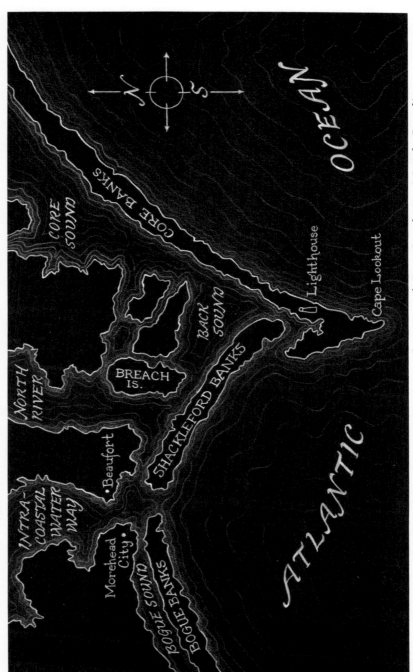

Breach Island and Shackleford Banks in the area of Cape Lookout, North Carolina

⚏Where the Spirits Walk

Breach Island, which is the setting of this story, lies halfway down the North Carolina Coast, cradled in the arms of two slender barrier islands. Shackleford Banks and Core Banks are the names of these arms; they link with other arms to form the long line of barrier islands known as the Outer Banks of North Carolina.

At its southern end, at Cape Lookout, the Core Banks arm elbows sharply into the vast and often wild Atlantic. Such elbows, or capes, are sculptured to this shape by stormy seas all over the world. Core's companion arm, Shackleford Banks, veers westward from Cape Lookout.

The sea erodes Shackleford's shoreline too, and beats at the marshy islets scattered in the sound behind it. These little "inner banks," however, ride out storms diminished by the Outer Banks. Fishermen who work the water around Breach routinely ignore foul weather. The Indians probably did so too, for centuries preceding them.

These were fishing islands long before the English colonized them. On Breach Island, all the roads are surfaced with oyster shells taken from a gigantic midden piled ten feet high, some say, by the Coree Indians who assembled there year after year for feasting.

Descendants of colonials inhabit Breach to this day, but the Corees no longer walk the land—except perhaps in spirit. They were a warrior people who succumbed long ago to equally warlike Indians, the Woccos.

We know little about the Coree woman, Crippled Swan, who survived her tribe's slaughter. Her husband may have been her rescuer as well—one Giles Guthrie, an Englishman whose forebears came to the Outer Banks during the reign of Elizabeth I.

Giles and Crippled Swan settled on Shackleford Banks, which then bordered (as it still does) the watery route of whales migrating north in early spring. Those were the days of a thriving whaling industry. Every part of a taken whale was used or sold—the flesh, the oil, the skin. Sailors carved ornaments from the teeth. Fishermen made and mended their nets with baleen needles. Manufacturers of whalebone corset stays prospered.

Diamond City, a whaling community near Cape Lookout's diamond-patterned lighthouse, flourished on Shackleford Banks during the 1800s. Giles and Crippled Swan, however, never dwelt in Diamond City. They lived instead at the other end of the Banks, on a distant rise known as Guthrie's Knob. Why did they so isolate themselves, on an already isolated island? We can only speculate. We do know that the society of the times frowned upon marriage between Anglo and Indian.

The lonely plight of Crippled Swan is particularly poignant. She had witnessed the destruction of her village, Cwareuuoc; she knew herself to be the last of the Corees. At Guthrie's Knob she lived in constant view of Breach Island, the ancient feasting ground of her people. Perhaps she took comfort in communing with their ghosts, for her tribe believed in spirits.

The Guthries who today live on Breach Island, where this story begins, speak proudly of their Coree blood, but the names of Giles and Crippled Swan have long been forgotten. Surprising? Think again. Not many Americans can recite the given names of all their great-grandparents.

1

☙ Fire on Shackleford!

"Savvy."

The girl on the sofa bed stirred beneath the sheet. She brushed irritably at the slippery black hair that slid across her cheek.

"Sa-a-avy."

Did somebody call her? Or did she dream somebody spoke her name, prying her out of the safety of sleep, dispatching her to the perils of wakefulness? For a moment she allowed herself to deny the summons, wherever it came from, to shape the demand into an agreeable postponement. But it didn't work. It never did. Savannah sat up with a groan, grudgingly conscious now and listening.

"Gone get you!" a voice threatened.

Savannah snickered. Pocosin, her little brother, babbling in his sleep again. She leaned toward the porch, where his cot was, and implored in a baby whisper, "Please don't eat me, Mr. Troll. Wait for the second Billy Goat Gruff, he's much bigger."

A short silence ensued. Poco seemed to be thinking over her suggestion. "Mussel shells," he mumbled at last.

"Conch shells," she fired back, but this time he did not respond. Poco never carried on a satisfactory conversation in his sleep. Savannah lay back down and studied the low ceiling.

Where the Guthries lived, secrets posted themselves like love letters through cracks in the uneven boards that formed the floor of her parents' bedroom overhead. Often Savannah could hear everything Mama and Daddy said to each other, talking over the day's events upstairs. The spring she was twelve, she learned the minute her mother did when the price of flounder finally, finally edged up and her father said well all right then, all right. He would buy them a TV, if that was what it took to keep peace in the family.

"Ayuh," Mama had exulted.

True to his word, Daddy had hitched a ride to Morehead, and he bought the small black-and-white set that now stood on the stout wooden table where they ate all their meals. They still checked the fuzzy Wilmington channel to get the tides schedule, and for trawlers' reports on the menhaden catch.

Alas, that was about all the good having a TV in the house did them. The blizzard on their screen snowed out all the soaps and game shows Mama had so counted on enjoying. Cable had not yet invaded their island, and an aerial tall enough to bring in a decent picture would cost him an arm and a leg, Daddy said; and he said he wasn't about to let Mama talk him into throwing more salt into the ocean.

All the same, if it weren't for Mama, who was very up-to-date in many respects, they would still be drawing water from a cistern, like Grammaw. Pocosin, being only eight, took indoor plumbing for granted, as something their family was entitled to. But Savannah did not so easily forget the smelly old privy modestly shrubbed by silverling and sweet bay on the path between the house and their boat dock. They had Mama to thank for the tiny modern bathroom crammed under their stairs. Daddy still grumbled that it was a luxury they didn't need, and cost too much besides.

Theirs was an ordinary fisherman's house, like many another on Breach Island, one room wide and two rooms tall. Savannah and Poco had both been born in the upstairs room.

A hundred years ago their house, single-storied then, had stood on Shackleford Banks, in the Indian settlement called Guthrie's Knob. When the big hurricane of 1899 washed seawater completely across the island, spoiling gardens and wrecking boats and houses, it drove the Guthries to the more sheltered "inner bank," Breach Island.

The entire population of Diamond City fled with them, floating their dwellings like so many houseboats across Back Sound. Diamond City memories

faded as the former whaling town slid farther and farther into the Atlantic. And so too did memories of
Guthrie's Knob recede, as old prejudices blurred in
the building of a new community.

To Savannah's house had been added, besides the
upstairs and the new bathroom, a side porch looking
toward Shackleford Banks. The porch had been en-
closed and fitted with windows only this summer,
when Daddy made some money on an Old Harkers
Island boat Dr. McWilliams bought off of him. Poco
had been sleeping on the porch since school started
last month. Mama said eight was too old for him to
still be sharing a bed with Savannah.

Savannah adored sleeping by herself. She could
sprawl over the entire bed which, unfolded, half filled
the living part of their downstairs room. No more
fights about her rolling over onto Poco's side. No
more waking up in a wet bed in the middle of the
night.

Sea oats rustled in the yard outside. A rising Oc-
tober breeze drifted through doors and windows,
all opened wide to invite it inside on this breathless
night. Shh-shh, the sea oats sighed. The waters of
Back Sound swished and sloshed in their basin. Shh-
shh, whispered the wind in its passage through the
screened doors and windows.

Savannah listened, separating the familiar night
sounds. She spoke into the darkness. "Poke?"

Poco shuffled across the bare floor toward the front
door.

Savannah climbed out of bed. "This way, Poke." She seized his shoulders and turned him toward the bathroom door.

"Um, um—*myself*," he snarled, and twisted free of her grasp.

Normally you couldn't ask for a sweeter little guy than Poco; but half awake like this he would fight with a shark's frenzy. She didn't dare let him go back to bed without draining him, for he would simply fall asleep again, and then he'd wet, but she felt too drowsy to argue with him. When she saw him wander into the bathroom, she returned to the sofa bed and slid under the sheet. She would just close her eyes for one little minute. Only until she heard the toilet flush, she told herself.

The next she knew, she had got out of bed, drawn by something, sensing something wrong. Had she heard the toilet flush? She couldn't think quite straight. Poco wasn't in the bathroom. He wasn't on the porch, either. Savannah passed her hands beneath his cot, located his sneakers there, his jeans and T-shirt lying in a heap on the floor with his ball and bat.

She padded back to her own room and searched shadowy corners, feeling along walls stippled with moonlight. Poco might have gone, as he sometimes did, to slip into bed with Mama and Daddy; but surely she would have heard the racket he made on the stairs, or Mama and Daddy, bawling him out.

She stood at the screen door for a moment nursing her resentment. Poco didn't mean to, of course, but he managed to mess up an awful lot, and it was always she, Savannah, who had to bail out the boat. Savannah it was who, night after night, got him up to go to the bathroom; who put him into fresh pajamas and changed the sheets when he wet them; and did he ever thank her the next day, or apologize? He did not. He acted unconcerned. He probably figured it was a big sister's job to look after him.

A mile away, across Back Sound, the Lookout light deliberately winked. Savannah numbered the seconds it took the beam to revolve between winks. One-menhaden, two-menhaden, three-menhaden. She counted fish to measure the seconds. Five menhaden later she saw, across Barden Inlet from the lighthouse, orange light beginning to finger the sky—fire on Shackleford!

The flames towered even as she watched. No fish-fry blaze, that one! The arsonist must have torched another fisherman's camp over there; this would make the third since September. One of these nights that same firebug might very well destroy the little overnight shelter Daddy had built for himself at Guthrie's Knob, on the other end of Shackleford.

Savannah clasped her arms across her chest and rocked back and forth, distraught. A terrible notion came to her, that Poco had something to do with this fire, those other fires, on Shackleford.

A movement outside diverted her, a shifting within the sea oats that grew down to the sound, but enough unlike their rhythmic nodding to draw her attention.

In the next instant she saw a furtive figure emerge from the tall grasses. A creature naked above the waist and sinister in the moonlight, slithered along the path to the boat dock. In its hand it carried a club.

She seized Poco's baseball bat to protect herself, if it came to that. The creature moved stealthily toward the boat dock. To her horror, she made out another figure on the path: fat little Poco, waddling along aimlessly, pausing to hitch up his pajamas. Instinctively she comprehended that it was Poco the creature was after. It crept along, all bent over, moving faster now, its club raised to shoulder height.

Savannah flew out the door, her own club ready. The creature turned to confront her, and she did not hesitate. With all her strength, she slammed her weapon across its skull. She felt the shattering crunch throughout her whole body, she saw the monster collapse and fall. "Ouf," she heard it moan.

"Run, Poco!" she croaked. "Run for the house!"

Poco turned around. He hitched his pajamas again. He did not run, but he did head for the house. He almost trod on the figure that lay crumpled in the path. He stopped short. His eyes, when he looked at Savannah, gleamed strange and vacant in the moonlight. He backed away and plunged into the sea oats to avoid approaching his sister and the fallen creature.

"Oh, Poco," said Savannah, "what have I done?"

2

A Signal from the Nightwalker

Brilliant light glared in her face. She threw up an arm to shield her eyes. On the sandy pathway some jagged object, probably a shell, stabbed her instep. She staggered.

"Savannah," her father said. "Honey. Are you all right?" His bare arm restrained her.

She fought to wrench away from him. She felt panicky and confused. The flashlight in his hand bored a pitiless light into her eyes.

"It's Daddy, honey. Daddy. It's Daddy," he repeated, with a monotony that maddened her.

But presently, unwillingly, she made herself focus on reality. "Daddy," she quavered. By what crazy trick of mind had she mistaken him for a monster? She could not believe what she had done. Clubbed her own father! Instinctively she sought both to confess and to deny.

"I thought you were somebody else . . . I mean, I was scared . . . I mean, where did Poco go? We've got to find Poco." With both hands she flailed at the light.

She couldn't collect her wits, with that glare accusing her.

Mercifully, her father dropped the beam from her face. "Poco's gone back inside," he said. "Are you all right?"

She could see her father's expression now, regarding her oddly and no wonder, after the blow she had dealt him. She covered her face with both hands. "I didn't go to hurt you, Daddy."

"You didn't hurt me. You caught me off-balance, was all. Don't you worry about me."

When she peeked through her fingers she saw her father still looking at her, whole and unbludgeoned as far as she could tell.

"What did you hit me with, anyway?" he asked.

She dropped her head. "Poco's bat."

"Poco's bat is made of plastic, Savannah. You couldn't possibly have hurt me with it, don't you see?"

She squeezed her eyes tight, like saying Amen to a fervent prayer. Maybe it was true that she hadn't hurt him, although she still couldn't quite believe it. She felt so spacy! She wondered uneasily what had become of the bat.

His arm supported her. "Let's sit down for a minute, let you get your land legs back."

His thick black hair fell carelessly across a broad forehead. Savannah could see that his smooth chest glistened, not with blood but sweat—that was the Coree in him. The people of his tribe piped steam through their veins, he sometimes boasted. Even in winter he never wore the tops to his pajamas.

"You okay now?" Daddy asked.

Savannah expelled a breath. "I guess so." She felt grateful for her father's solid presence there on the porch step beside her. Her mind still churned sluggishly, figuring a way to explain. "I thought I saw somebody out here trying to get Poco," she said at last. "Somebody holding a club."

"It was me," said her father. "The club you saw was only my flashlight. I probably heard Poco leave the house the same time you did."

She said, "I guess he went walking in his sleep again."

"Yes. Tomorrow I'll move the screen hook up out of his reach. We can't have him prowling around the island all hours of the night." He sat for a moment in silence, looking out at the night. "Another fire on Shackleford," he said, and added bitterly, "One by one, they're driving us off our ground."

"Who's doing it, Daddy?"

"The feds, the U.S. Park Service, you ought to know that by now. They're going to make a national seashore out of Shackleford."

"Yes, I know, but I mean, who's been burning the shacks?"

He snorted. "The nightwalker, maybe. That's what my people would have called that kind of mischief. A night spirit."

Daddy's people. Savannah could just barely remember her grandfather, a fisherman like the rest of the Guthries. "Grandpa Guthrie believed in spirits?" she asked.

"I never heard *him* say so exactly, but it's what his tribe told, about most anything they couldn't explain. The Corees wouldn't have seen anything unusual about Poco walking in his sleep: they'd have said he was hunting for his spirit."

"Why would he do that?"

Some people—and not only the Indians—went through life searching for peace of mind, Daddy said. The Corees believed that the nightwalker literally wandered the earth, seeking reunion with its human body. Perhaps it longed for wholeness to redeem its dark nature.

Sometimes Daddy talked like the preacher in their church, Savannah thought, listening. Daddy was pretty religious.

Daddy said, "What happened in their sleep was very real to those old Corees. Well, to me, too—it's only afterward that I can't make sense out of my dreams. I guess most folks feel that way."

"Sometimes I can't tell the part I dream from what's real," Savannah said. She waved toward Shackleford. "I know I was still half asleep, but I got the craziest idea that Poco had something to do with the fire over there."

Her father said mysteriously, "Maybe we all do."

"What do you mean?"

"Maybe it's our nightwalkers, sending us a signal."

"Signal about what?"

He gave her a bracing little hug. "That it's time to go in. What do you say we both get off to bed?"

She hung behind for a moment to search the grasses just beyond the step, wanting to locate the missing bat. Her father called from inside, "Coming, Savvy? What are you looking for out there?"

"Nothing," said Savannah.

*

She awoke obsessed about the bat. She realized it was only a toy, but since last night it had become a sinister toy. She remembered dropping it on the path; and then, mysteriously, it had vanished. And for all her father's unconcern, she still didn't feel right about last night—those baffling fires on Shackleford, for instance. That awful moment when she believed she had struck down a monster.

Her unease mingled poorly with the comfortable Saturday smell of pancakes and yaupon tea. Mama had figured out a way to use her Mr. Coffee machine for brewing the yaupon holly leaves that Grammaw dried for their family every spring. All for modern, Mama was. Grammaw steeped her tea in a chowder pot.

At breakfast, Mama said, "Savannah, you're not eating your pancakes. Would you like an egg? Bacon? Eat some of Grammaw's good fig preserves, why

don't you?" Nobody could accuse Mama of setting a
stingy table.

"I'm not very hungry this morning," Savannah said.

Poco said, "I'll eat her pancakes if she doesn't want
them."

Savannah shoved back from the table. "Fat," she
muttered, to shift her guilt onto Poco.

Poco joined her on the path outside, oblivious to
her mood, his round puppy face cheerful. "What are
you looking for?" he asked.

"Nothing."

"You look like you're looking for something," he
said. He began combing the grasses on either side of
the path. "Tell me what it is and I'll help you look."

"Nothing, I told you."

"If it's nothing, how come you keep looking?"

"Maybe I'm trying to find the same thing you were
hunting last night."

Poco's face crumpled. He said, frightened, "I wasn't
hunting anything."

"Then what were you doing out here, in the middle
of the night?"

He appeared visibly to shrivel, pudgy little Poco. "I
wasn't—I didn't—" he faltered. It took so little to
wipe out Poco.

She knew it was hateful of her to tease him about
the nighttime wanderings that he couldn't help, and
furthermore couldn't recollect. She gave her brother
an apologetic shove. "Only kidding, Poke," she said.

"Why don't you go get your ball and bat and I'll pitch you a few."

"I don't know where my bat is."

"Look on the porch, beside your bed. That's where you always leave it."

"I don't neither, always." He shoveled a sneakered toe into the sandy path.

"That's where I saw it last."

"Well, it's not there now." But he added, brightening, "My ball's there. We'll practice throwing curves, want to?"

"Fine, Poke."

He ran to fetch the ball and Savannah continued to part the yellowing, nodding grasses. The bat had to be here somewhere. If not, who (or what?) had spirited it away? The nightwalker?

3

The Ditdot's Secret Staircase

On the ferry side of Breach Island, the slightly elevated portion that lay across a brackish river from the mainland, the island's prosperous mowed their lawns and fenced and bordered them with the familiar shrubs of North Carolina's coastal savannahs—oleander, juniper, crotons, hydrangea. On the Guthries' side of the island, sea oats and spartina grass mantled the flat land separating their house from the waters of Back Sound.

"You never see ducks and geese over by Fulcher's anymore," Savannah's father often declared. "Nothing for them to feed on." Nobbled hillocks of drained sludge now stood where marsh grasses once flourished. Before Kin Fulcher dredged for his docks, Daddy said, ducks and geese and swans used to flock there by the thousands, on their way south. Daddy had practically grown up on stewed swan.

In another month, Savannah would fall asleep at night to the incessant honking and quacking of migrating waterfowl overhead. Her family would eat roast mallard for Thanksgiving, a welcome change from their daily diet of fish. But the time was coming, her father warned, when they'd forget what it was to sit down to a fine Christmas goose, or a supper of gooseliver sausage, or whippoorwill peas seasoned with duck fat.

Bemused, Savannah stood on the path and surveyed the stretch of sea oats stubble adjoining the Guthries. Daddy had long coveted the Evangelicals' property next door. That land combined with his would have given him enough frontage to build a small marina on the sound. During the summer, the Evangelicals had voted to build a new parsonage, and had put the old one on the market. The chance Daddy had been waiting for! It appeared that he might actually get his marina.

Then disappointment struck. Dr. McWilliams, who lived in Raleigh, had topped his bid for the sprawling residence and had promptly begun fixing it up as a vacation cottage. Mrs. McWilliams came down from Raleigh with a decorator. The electricians arrived next with the plumbers from Morehead, and after them, swarms of carpenters, masons, and painters.

The whole McWilliams family had spent the previous weekend scything down sea oats and transplanting runners of centipede grass to start a lawn. Savannah's father had stamped back and forth outside, carrying on a loud one-sided conversation about ditdots who paved over the mainland and then wouldn't be content until they scalped the coastal lands as well.

"Would you like me to show you my room?"

The pert voice behind her spun Savannah around. A girl about her age stood on the path. She wore blue eyeshadow. She also wore yellow satin running shorts and a blue T-shirt that urged in darker blue lettering, *Save Shackleford!* Her yellow hair frizzed out from beneath a navy fisherman's cap stenciled with the same plea: *Save Shackleford!*

You could tell a ditdot from a Breacher by these caps and tees. All the uplanders wore them. They called themselves Environmentalists. Kincaid Fulcher said they were getting up a petition to drive the fishermen off Shackleford.

"Well, do you want to see my room or not?" the girl demanded.

Savannah gave the blue T-shirt an insolent once-over. "Where is your room?" she asked. "On Shackleford?"

"No, silly, it's over there." The girl pointed at the parsonage. "That's our house now."

"Oh. Then I guess you're Mary Lou McWilliams."

"Mary Jean," the girl corrected. "What's your name?"

"Savannah."

"How old are you?"

None of your business, Savannah felt like answering. Breachers didn't pry, and they didn't appreciate ditdot prying; already, Grammaw would have said, this girl smelled fishy.

"I'm twelve," Savannah finally allowed.

Mary Jean said, "I'm going on twelve. That makes me almost as old as you. I'll be in seventh grade next year. Are you in seventh yet?"

Savannah acknowledged this with a grudging nod.

"Was that your little brother out here with you a while ago? What's his name?"

You could also tell a ditdot by the way they continually tried to start a conversation. "Poco," Savannah said after a long moment. One answer at a time would do for Miss Meddle.

Mary Jean said "Poco? That's Spanish for *little,* isn't it? I'm learning Spanish this year in my school. You call him Poco because he's little, right?"

"Wrong. We call him Poco for short. His whole name is Pocosin."

"*Pocosin?* What kind of a name is that?"

"It's Coree. The Indian word for swamp; one that's got a whole bunch of trees and vines and stuff growing in it." Savannah gestured. "Like the land across the road."

Mary Jean yelped in derision. "He's named after a swamp? Your folks named their kid after a *swamp?*"

Savannah said, "For your information, Indians around here depended on the pocosins for shelter and food and medicine. They respected the land. Indians would never mow down the sea oats and wreck the marshlands the way the white people do, my father says." She added, spacing her words, "My father is Coree Indian."

Daddy was only one-sixteenth Indian, but he was one hundred percent proud of that fraction. Proud enough to name both his children after the land he worshipped, his son for the Indian word that meant bog-on-a-hill, his daughter for the grassy pine savannahs.

Behind them the screen door banged and Poco ran from the house brandishing his bat. "I found it, Savannah!" he yelled. He pounded up to where the two girls stood. "It was in the laundry hamper," he said, and handed the bat to Savannah. His mouth hung open in a wide grin. Poco was like Mama's side of the family. He and Mama and Grammaw all showed a lot of tongue when they smiled.

"Hey there, Pocahontas," said Mary Jean.

Poco scowled. "My name's not Pocahontas," he informed her. "Pocahontas was a girl."

"Well, you run like a girl," said Mary Jean. "Oh! Now I see why. Look at the Donald Duck feet, I wish you would."

Poco looked down at feet that paddled absurdly outward, like diving flippers.

Mary Jean said, "Can't you see, dopey? You've put your sneakers on the wrong feet."

Poco shot her a snide glance. "They're the only feet I've got." He drilled the ball at her. She fired it back with a precision that made him blink.

Savannah's earlier anxiety about the bat slipped

neatly into sarcasm. "And just what was your bat doing in the laundry hamper?" she asked.

The boy wilted. "I don't know."

"How did you happen to find it, then? The laundry hamper is no place to keep a bat. What made you think to look for it there?"

Mary Jean interceded. "Get off his case, Savannah. He found the bat, didn't he? What difference does it make to you where?"

Poco regarded his new champion gratefully. He said to Mary Jean, "You want to throw me some curves and see if I can hit them?"

"You can't throw curves with a Wiffle ball," she objected. "And a Wiffle bat is for babies. I tell you what, Poco, my brother's got real bats, wooden, metal, you name it, Jeff's got it. Next trip we make to Breach, I'll bring along a real bat and give you some batting practice. Okay? But right now I'm going to show Savannah my room. Okay?"

Typical Okay ditdot, Savannah noted; Okay every other sentence.

She gave Poco's bat a quick check before handing it over to him. It hadn't split or cracked; she couldn't find even a dent on it. She must have imagined the violent blow across Daddy's skull, or perhaps magnified it, the way she would in a dream.

"Come on, Savannah," Mary Jean coaxed. She moved in close and confided, "My room's got a secret staircase. I bet you can't figure out where it is."

She could go next door long enough to find the secret staircase, Savannah decided; she loved a mystery. Also, she wouldn't mind checking out the rumors about the remodeling that had gone on next door. Grammaw said Mr. Wade, the grocer, reported wall-to-wall carpeting upstairs and down. Grammaw still scrubbed her wooden floors with a stone, the way her own mother had, and sprinkled the silvery wood with clean white sand.

As they pushed through the overgrown yaupon hedge between their two houses, Mary Jean inquired idly, "What about your name, Savannah? I know that's an Indian word. Did your folks name you after the city?"

"No, of course not," said Savannah. "The city's named after me."

4

New Friend, Old Enemy

"All right, show me where the secret staircase is."

Mary Jean flopped on one of the twin beds, giggling. "If I showed you, it wouldn't be a secret!"

"You don't have to tell. It won't be a secret for long, with me." Savannah circled the room purposefully. She rapped on all the walls and listened for a telltale difference in resonance. Not for nothing had she read all the mystery books in the school library. Knock-knock-knock—

"Come in," said a man's voice. Dr. McWilliams stood in the doorway.

Savannah stopped knocking and hid her hands behind her back, like a little kid caught out. She hated being surprised.

The doctor said, "Knocking for me to come in or you to come out?" Heavy horn-rimmed glasses enlarged the twinkle of his gray eyes.

"Neither one," Savannah muttered. "I was hunting for the secret staircase."

"What secret staircase?"

Mary Jean squealed "Dadd*eeee!*" and Dr. Mc-Williams blinked his way into a double-take. He said, "Oh. *That* secret staircase."

Savannah said, "So there isn't one, after all."

"Yes there is too! There is so a secret staircase!" Mary Jean jumped up and grabbed her father around the neck. She sputtered something in his ear that made him smile. "Don't tell!" she warned. "Now you tell Savannah there is a secret staircase in my room."

"You said I wasn't to tell," he teased.

"Daddy! You know what I mean. Go on. Tell her it's true."

"It's true, Savannah," said Dr. McWilliams. "There really is a secret staircase." The fake solemnity didn't suit him, any more than the maroon T-shirt he wore (*Save Shackleford!*). Dr. McWilliams looked like he belonged in a three-piece suit. He offered his hand. "How do you do, Savannah."

"Scuse me. I forgot," said Mary Jean. She presented her visitor with aplomb. "This is Savannah, Daddy, from next door."

"So I guessed." The doctor shuffled Savannah's fingers in his, like a deck of cards. "Have you always bitten your nails, Savannah?"

None of your business, she wanted to tell him. He was as meddlesome as his daughter. Worse. Oh, much worse! She was thunderstruck to hear him ask Mary Jean, in the most casual way, "Did you have a good bowel movement this morning, sweetie?"

Mary Jean didn't seem in the least perturbed. "Not very," she replied and proceeded to describe her body's function so fully that Savannah wished she could vanish, listening to her. She felt her own body grow hot all over.

"I want you to start eating bran cereal for breakfast," said the doctor, taking his leave. "I think you need more fiber in your diet. Listen, don't you girls go out this morning without your hats; the sun is like the middle of August. Take care of your skin now, so I don't have to take care of it later. Put on sun block— well, perhaps you needn't, Savannah, with that olive complexion."

He turned back and peered with interest into her face. He seized her chin, he turned her head to one side and inspected her profile. "Mm-hm," he said. "Indian?"

"Part," said Savannah.

"Thought so," said the doctor.

"Does he always act like that?" she asked Mary Jean, after Dr. McWilliams had gone.

"Like what?"

"Like—you know, asking about my fingernails and if I was Indian—all those *personal* questions. Doesn't that embarrass you? When he talks about your, uh, your . . . ?"

"My b.m.'s? Nah. Don't pay any attention to Daddy. He's a pediatrician. Everybody that isn't thirty years old, practically, Daddy talks to like they're his patients. You won't notice it after you get used to him."

She would always notice, Savannah decided. She would *never* get used to discussing her bowel movement, even with a doctor. Not even if the doctor was her own father.

"Hey, do you like Kristi Valenti?" Mary Jean pulled a record from the rack on top of the bookcase and turned up the volume of her player. "Here's her latest, *Swimmin' Wimmin*. It's my fave." She closed her eyes in rapture. "Will you listen to that Kristi beg? Is she ever wired!"

Savannah, dazzled, agreed. Definitely wired.

Thick blue carpeting covered the entire floor of Mary Jean's room. The woodwork had been painted and the walls papered in Mary Jean's favorite colors, blue and yellow. Curtains matched the chair cushions, framed prints of horses hung on the walls. Until this morning, Savannah had never thought much about walls, except as a sort of storage place where you hung nets and waterproofs on hooks to drain in summer, and toboggans and insulated jackets in winter. The only picture on the Guthries' wall showed a topsail coasting schooner on a calendar given out by Kincaid Fulcher, Fish Dealer.

"You want to stay for lunch?" said Mary Jean. "I'll go ask Aurora if we can eat up here."

Mary Jean wore a teen bra under that T-shirt, Savannah discovered in her absence. Not that she was snooping! Mary Jean said she could look anywhere she wanted to, for the button to the secret staircase that was bound to be concealed somewhere in this room. Savannah searched the closet and looked through the bureau drawers. In the vanity she found three shapely, lacy bras stacked beside a box of MaxiThins.

Savannah forgot about the secret staircase. She touched the unpromising front of her own faded shirt. Then she looked at the cosmetics lined up on the vanity's surface: lipstick, blusher, nail polish, styling mousse. Mary Jean wasn't even twelve years old yet!

Oh, but it was an elegant room and, apart from that ridiculous grown-up stuff, filled with intriguing junk—pads of drawing paper and colored chalks on the table, a guitar in one corner, a rag doll nearly as tall as Mary Jean lounging in another, stuffed animals standing about on the windowsills, jigsaw puzzles and games sharing the bookshelves with a collection of paperbacks. The room of a princess.

Savannah could see why her father hankered for this place. Up until now she had not appreciated his longing to build his own marina, or his frustration each time he turned up too late and too short of money to buy the frontage he needed.

Grammaw said Daddy wouldn't have let go of the cash, anyway, close as he was with his money. But he *had* made an offer, when the parsonage first came onto the market. If only he hadn't decided the asking price was too high; if only he hadn't waited for the Evangelicals to lower it. To think, Savannah mourned, this luxurious room might have been hers!

"Aurora wants to go out in the boat with Dad," Mary Jean reported, returning with a trayload of provisions, "so we have to make our own lunch. But we can go get ice cream for dessert. Aurora gave me the money."

"Who's Aurora?"

"My mother. Mom. Her first name is Aurora."

Savannah tried to imagine calling Mama by her first name. Bessie. "I never knew anybody named Aurora," she said.

"It's meant to sound artistic. Aurora's an artist. On her side everybody's very artistic. Do you want butter on your sandwich or mayo?"

"Oh, mayo, I guess," said Savannah carelessly. She was beginning to like Mary Jean's style.

*

At the Creamy Queen, Kincaid Fulcher, Junior, dispensed soft ice cream with a flourish, and the girls carried their cones off to a vacant booth.

"Wow," said Mary Jean. "This is twice as big as the cones they give in Raleigh."

Savannah smirked. "It's twice what they give here, too." Kinky Fulcher's reaction to her sophisticated new friend had not escaped her notice.

"What do you mean by that?"

"Nothing," said Savannah. Behind her she could hear Kinky loudly bragging to Euel Jennings about the big bucks he had been drawing from his Saturday job here at the Creamy Queen.

A moment later he stood beside their booth, proffering the hot fudge kettle. "You'erns wanna free dip?"

"No thanks," said Savannah curtly. She could easily do without any favors from Kinky Fulcher.

"How about you, buttercup? No charge," Kinky urged Mary Jean.

The younger girl said primly, "I don't care for any, thank you."

Watching Kinky return to his post, Mary Jean said, "What's with that dude? Anybody you know? I think he acts kind of weird."

If Mary Jean only knew how weird. But Savannah wasn't ready to dish up the dirt on her old enemy, Kinky Fulcher. "He's in my grade at school," she said without inflection.

"In your grade? But he's huge!"

"He got left back a couple of times."

"Figures. Are there any cute boys in your grade?"

"Some," said Savannah. She wondered if Mary Jean would consider Euel Jennings cute. Most of the girls in seventh thought he was a hunk. (He was!) But she herself was not the least bit boy crazy, and she had no intention of getting that way.

"Do all the kids around here talk funny? I don't

mean you," said Mary Jean. "You talk just regular, but that creep at the counter, and the other boy talking to him, they sound . . . you know, different."

Savannah found herself defending Kinky Fulcher, of all people. "It's because they still talk like the first settlers on the Outer Banks," she informed Mary Jean. "A lot of folks on Breach, they go back to when Queen Elizabeth was queen in England, and they still talk like she did. My teacher says we should be proud of the way our ancestors talked. The language of Shakespeare, she says."

"Groovy," said Mary Jean.

Kinky swaggered up beside their booth once more. "You'erns gotcher English signment done, Savannah?" He explained for Mary Jean's benefit, "Me and Savannah got the same teacher in school, see, and we're posed to write a piece about our town—summat loike thet. My folks being big around here— Fulchers is my folks—Oi figger Savannah'd thank me, did Oi hope her out."

"I don't need any help," Savannah told him.

Mary Jean asked, on their way back, "Just how big are Mr. Bigshot's folks around here?"

"Pretty big," Savannah admitted. Kincaid Fulcher, Fish Dealer, might not come off big by Raleigh standards, but the family did go way back, and nearly every fisherman on the island dealt with the firm. Kincaid Fulcher had started out with nothing more than a buy boat. Now the trawlers came to his docks.

Fulcher it was who set the price on flounder, shrimp, oysters, blue crabs, hard clams, scallops.

But why should Fulcher be the one to say? Savannah wondered. Her daddy knew more about fish and fishing than Kinky's; and the Guthries went just as far back as Fulchers—farther; because Daddy's people, the Corees, fished and hunted on Breach maybe hundreds of years before Fulchers ever thought of coming there.

Mary Jean said, "You want to sleep over tonight? Aurora said I can invite you, but we have to make our own supper. She and Daddy are going out for dinner."

"Don't you want to go with them?"

"Nah. We eat out all the time. I'd rather stay home and fool around the kitchen. Are you up for that?"

"Yeah, sure. I have to go tell my mother first, is all."

But telling Mama, Savannah suspected, might not blow as breezy as she made it sound. Sleeping over at the ditdot's!

5

⚘ Cozzing Up to the McWilliamses

Mama said, "Where have you been all morning? Poco said you went off with that McWilliams girl next door. I sent him over for you, at dinnertime, but nobody was home, so we went ahead and ate."

"That's okay," said Savannah. "I didn't want any lunch."

Mama dried her hands on her apron. "You weren't hungry for breakfast either," she said. "You're not catching cold, are you? This is changy weather."

"No, Mama. What I meant, I wouldn't have wanted but just a little snack, anyway—"

Mama said, "I left you some hush puppies on the stove." She swooped across the room to peel back Savannah's eyelid for inspection. She prodded her chest. She prodded her stomach. "I bet you're about to come sick," she said.

"Period, Mama," said Savannah. "People don't say come sick anymore. They say period."

"Talk us some more ditdot gab, why don't you? I

say you're of age for it, however they want to call it."
With a wise smile, Mama caressed the lacquered
blond curls of her hairdo.

Savannah said, "Mama! I haven't got my period,
and furthermore I don't care if I never get it."

But she couldn't resist confiding in Mama. "Mary
Jean gets hers, though, Mama! She told me she started
in August, and she's not even twelve yet. She wears a
bra, too, but not all the time. When she wears a T-
shirt without one, she pastes Band-Aids over so her
front doesn't—you know, show pointy."

Mama laughed widely, her broad tongue glistening.

Through some happy chance, Savannah had hit on
exactly the right gab to soften Mama up. By the time
she got around to asking permission to sleep over,
Mama said, "Well, Savvy, I don't see much wrong of
it. A girl needs somebody their own age to talk to. If
I hadn't of, I guess I'd be stoning the floor in your
Grammaw's house till yet."

With Daddy, however, Savannah didn't slip so easily through the net. He was sitting on the stoop grind-
ing down a nick in a scallop knife when she made
the mistake of maneuvering past him. Naturally he
wanted to know where she thought she was heading,
with her pajamas and toothbrush.

"I don't like you cozzing up to McWilliamses," he
growled, when she told him.

"Mama said it was all right."

"Does your mama think it's all right for them to

grab off all the land around here? Drive up prices on everything else so a man can't afford to work the water anymore?"

Savannah knew what he meant. Milk cost nearly double in the grocery store now, and Mr. Wade had put in a special shelf marked Gourmet Foods right up by the cash register. "It's not Mary Jean's fault, Daddy," she argued. "Mary Jean wouldn't even know what you're talking about."

"She never will," Daddy snapped. "McWilliamses aren't our kind of folks, and I don't want you going over there."

Daddy had a temper and he seldom bothered to control it: Coree blood was fighting blood. Even so, Savannah knew he could listen to reason. The Guthries had their indoor toilet and a bottle-gas stove, Daddy's temper notwithstanding, just from Mama knowing how to reason with him.

"Dr. McWilliams is nice, Daddy," Savannah wheedled. "Mary Jean's nice, too. She got a real good sense of humor."

"They're not our kind," Daddy repeated.

Savannah thought of something. "What's our kind?" she questioned. "Aren't we Americans, good as them? That's what you said about your people, the ones way back, that the white folks in Diamond City made live at Guthrie's Knob."

Daddy turned on her, and he looked so angry that there for a moment Savannah thought he might be going to whack her one. But he didn't. It was a funny thing: Daddy had the temper, but Mama did the whacking, whenever Savannah or Poco had it coming. Indians did not beat their children, according to Daddy.

"All right!" he grumped. "Be offen you, then, since you're so blame stuck on the ditdots."

The ease of her triumph alarmed her. She said, "If you really don't want me to, Daddy—"

"Go on, go on," he insisted. "I'm not trying to keep you. Besides, you'll likely be the only one on Breach Island ever to get the good out of a ditdot."

*

But letting her go didn't mean Daddy thought any better of the McWilliamses. Back home on Sunday night when Savannah sat down, bleary-eyed, to re-copy her English composition, she heard his pacing upstairs and caught the gist of his conversation with Mama.

"I don't like her *mumble mumble mumble,*" said Daddy, "and *mumble* the dingbatter snobs."

Mama said, in her very carrying voice, "Would you ruther her run around with that simple Wade young'ern, they have to keep a bib on her? Or the Fulcher girl, that already lets the boys feel her up? Savannah belongs to have one nice friend."

"*Mumble mumble!*" said Daddy. "*Mumble* a nice ditdot friend!"

But Savannah also heard the reassuring twang of

springs as Daddy sat on the side of the bed. She heard one boot drop, and then another. "A Visit to My Room," she wrote at the top of her paper.

She propped her chin in her palm and stared down at the swimming words of her title. She and Mary Jean had scarcely slept at all last night. Twice Mrs. McWilliams had come to shush them, when they got to giggling too loud. Mary Jean was a stitch! She would say any outrageous thing that popped into her head.

"Tomorrow," Savannah informed her pencil. She would do a better job after a good night's sleep. She could copy her composition on the ferryboat tomorrow, on her way to school.

*

Flames dotted Shackleford. Four huge fires—that meant four more shacks gone! And who had set them ablaze? She sensed that she must find some way of putting out the fires, before they reached Daddy's fishing shack. The tide was just beginning to come in; the water was no more than knee deep, out where Daddy moored the skiff. She and Poco had paddled and poled the shallow mile across to Shackleford Banks a number of times, just for the fun of it or, occasionally, to take Daddy a hot lunch.

The cold water, when she stepped into it, shocked her into rethinking the wisdom of trying to put out a fire that was clear across Back Sound. It was while she hesitated, shivering, that she fancied she saw some-

*body sitting in the skiff, a figure with its back to her,
hunched over in a waiting posture. It seemed deliberately to turn, with the intent of coming after her, and
she almost saw its face. She did not linger to risk the
vision of that evil countenance.*

She flew back to the house. She leaped into bed and
pulled the quilt over her head. She could have yelled
for help, she realized but she wouldn't have known
how to explain what it was she feared, why she had
gone down to the landing in the middle of the night,
and the more she thought about it, the more unsure
she became that she had seen anything at all in the
boat. Did I dream that? she wondered, sitting up in
her bed. Then she heard the screen door click as Poco
slipped inside.

She got up and went to confront him on the porch.
"That was you in the boat, wasn't it?" she accused.

His eyes glowed strangely in the darkness.

She shook his arm. "Was that you down at the
landing? Sitting in the skiff?" The eerie sense came
over her again, that Poco had something to do with
the fires on Shackleford Banks.

He jerked free of her grasp and struck clumsily at
her. Savannah heard the delicate rattle of some small
objects that flew from his hand onto the wooden
floor.

The bedroom door opened upstairs and Daddy's
voice said irritably, "Savannah. Poco. What's going on
down there?"

"Nothing, Daddy." She said, "We were just up looking at the fires over on Shackleford."

Her father came down the stairs in his bare feet for a look.

"We're scared they're going to burn your fish camp."

"Nobody but me is going to burn *my* shack, I guarantee you. How come this porch door is open?"

"I must have forgotten to latch it, when I went to bed." She gave her brother a shove. "Go to the bathroom, Poco."

After her father went back upstairs, Savannah knelt and ran her hands across the floor at the foot of her sofa bed. Her fingers located two blunt-nosed wooden splinters of familiar shape: kitchen matches. She padded her way in the dark to slip them into a metal holder fastened on the wall beside Mama's stove.

When she folded her bed back into the sofa the next morning, she found three more matches lying beneath it. She gathered them up and hastened to add them to the others in the holder. They were all, every one of them, ordinary blue-tip kitchen matches. Commoner than clams, Grammaw would say. Had it been common household matches that started those decidedly uncommon fires?

6

The Stranger on the Ferryboat

On the ferry the next morning Savannah went at once into the vacant canteen. Dooby Fulcher, the ferry master, never bothered to open his snack bar for the meager trade of the school crowd. Any real money came from off-islanders, on the return trip.

She had just finished copying her composition at a table beside the sea-etched window when the door opened and a man in a navy insulated jacket stepped inside. He wore a plaid flannel shirt beneath the jacket, with thermals showing at the neck, like one of the locals. He also wore boots and a peaked camouflage cap with the earflaps turned up, but his jacket was new and his pants were creased, and nobody on the ferry would have taken him for a true high tider.

"Hey there!" said the stranger.

Savannah laid a finger on the paper to mark her place before she raised her head. Adults riding the ferry would sometimes respect your homework, if you made it obvious.

Six varnished chairs with attached desk arms lined the opposite wall of the canteen and two tall stools stood empty at the counter, but this man chose to sit in a wooden chair across the tiny table from Savannah.

"That was some fire last night, wasn't it?" he remarked, in the bluff manner Savannah associated with uplanders. "Didn't you see it?" he asked, when Savannah neglected to respond.

Savannah shook her head, barely. She fitted her composition carefully into her folder and assembled her books.

The man persisted. "Hear about it?"

Savannah muttered, "I don't know about any fire." She stood up.

"Wait a minute," said the man. He reached inside his jacket, fingered a small, squarish wallet from his shirt pocket, and thumbed it open. His picture, in color, scowled at her from inside the wallet. An embossed seal fractured the signature underneath. The lines of close print below the signed picture scarcely registered on Savannah, stunned as she was by the bold printing across the bottom of his identity card:

Federal Bureau of Investigation.

"Now, I can see your folks have warned you against talking to strangers," said the man approvingly, "but I feel sure they'd want you to share any information you have with an agent of the Bureau." He continued to nod, persuasively. "So, maybe you heard your folks talking about the fire? Or maybe you'd feel more comfortable telling me what your friends have to say about it?"

The F.B.I.! Savannah went cold all over. "I don't know anything, I told you!" But she realized her panic was a dead giveaway and wouldn't, in any case, protect Poco. "We never even know about the fires till we see the fish camps burning, over there," she pleaded.

The man returned the wallet to his pocket. "I was talking about the Headquarters fire, last night. Wondered if you heard your folks mention it."

Savannah clutched her books to her chest—Headquarters?

The Park Service Headquarters, he said, down by the boat launch. And the excursion boat itself, burned to the gunwales and sunk in the water. Last night about midnight.

"Oh yes," he said, "the Shackleford fires are part and parcel of this whole enterprise. Somebody's putting us on notice, we realize that. We can live with a few shacks burned. But the excursion boat and Headquarters—now, that's different; that's *government property*." He paused to scan her face.

Savannah tried to make her expression blank. Oh, what had Poco got himself into this time? She shuffled her books and reached for the doorknob. "I don't know anything," she said again. Her voice came out high and whiny.

The man followed her onto the deck where most of the kids from middle and high school were standing around in their usual gangs. It seemed to Savannah, raw and acute from the news of this different arson, arson of *government property*, that everybody turned to look at her when she walked out of the canteen. She imagined that they fell silent as she made her way to the railing. She gripped the cold moist pipe. She gulped the whipping wind in deep, starved lungfuls. Her mouth felt dry.

Farther down the deck the stranger leaned on the railing beside Euel Jennings. "Hey there," she heard him say to Euel. "That was some fire down at Headquarters last night. Did you see it at all?" She saw Euel shake his head.

*

The story seared through school and crackled in Savannah's classroom. Even the off-islanders knew about it; the *Lookout* had run pictures of the catastrophe all over its front page.

Kinky Fulcher arrived at school late, after lunch, bragging about how he had slickered the F.B.I. man by pretending to know something about the arson. The agent had hustled him off the ferry, but a call to Kincaid Fulcher quickly verified his suspicion of Kinky's frivolous claim. After the man left, Kinky said, his old man had beat him good for the deception, but it had been worth it.

"I missed all of math and English and most of lunch

period, and got better grub in the canteen besides," he crowed.

Ms. Paisley said, "This is a perfectly dreadful deed for you to be boasting about, Kinky."

He said, with false sincerity, "Oh yes, ma'am. I know I done wrong."

Kinky had, in fact, worked late at the docks the previous night for his father, he said. He'd been loading ice and packers onto trawlers all during the time of the fire.

Ms. Paisley said, "What you did is called Obstruction of Justice, Kinky. Your foolish prank may very well have given the real culprit time to escape."

"Yes ma'am. I ain't never going to do nothing like that ever again," Kinky assured her.

Savannah thought of Poco and the blue-tip kitchen matches. Kinky's stupid prank had let Poco escape, Ms. Paisley said. Could she bear to be indebted to Kinky Fulcher?

Grammaw was burning with excitement, when Savannah stopped in at her house that afternoon. You could push Breachers just so far, Grammaw said; now it was the federals' turn to get singed.

"You'll see a ditdot scorched too, before the year's out," she promised. "Things'll die down before the next burning, but then—watch out!"

Grammaw cinched her apron for emphasis. "A hundred thousand dollars, this time, gone up in smoke!" And there wasn't anybody on the island sorry to see it go, she chortled.

Park Headquarters hadn't been much of a head-quarters—no more than a prefab utility building where a woman in a Smokey Bear hat gave out maps of Cape Lookout National Seashore and sold tickets to day-trippers during the summer season. The excursion boat, which lumbered between Breach and Shackleford, accounted for the big loss. It, too, was government property as the F.B.I. man had said.

Savannah walked home deeply distressed by Grammaw's vengeful tirade. Poco wasn't out for revenge on anybody. Poco didn't even know he'd been sleepwalking. But how did you go about explaining a mistake to an outfit as big and unforgiving as the federal government?

A notice of reward for information leading to arrest of the arsonist went up in the post office. Newspaper reporters interviewed the customers at Wade's store. Mary Jean's mother said, when they came down on Friday, that the unfortunate incident illuminated the dissatisfaction of Breach Island residents and their obvious need for a rigorous Park policy regarding land management on Shackleford.

"What we need more is a vigorous policy on dit-dots," Daddy said, when he heard about Mrs. McWilliams's statement.

But already the excitement was dying down. No arrests had been made. At Wade's the regulars winked and told one another the fire must have been an accident. It couldn't have been set to make a point, because who ever heard of getting a point across to the federals? It seemed clear that no one was going to claim the reward advertised in the post office.

"If somebody like Poco did it," Savannah said to Mary Jean, "would they put him in jail, do you reckon?"

"Why do you ask that?" Mary Jean wanted to know. "Poco's a decent little mutt. He wouldn't pull a stunt like that."

Savannah treaded water. "I didn't mean Poco; I meant, would they arrest some little kid, if he did it, and put him in jail?"

Mary Jean said shrewdly, "You didn't say *some little kid* at first, you said *Poco*. You think he knows something, don't you?"

That Mary Jean! Savannah might have guessed she couldn't put anything past her. Still, Mary Jean was her friend; they told each other everything, and she trusted her.

"The thing is, Poco walks in his sleep sometimes," she confided, "and I don't always know what he's been up to."

"If that's all, you don't have to worry," Mary Jean said. "Sleepwalkers don't go around setting fires. They come a lot closer to hurting themselves than they do anybody else."

"Well, Poco has done some pretty queer things."

Mary Jean gave her a dig in the ribs. "Are you sure queer doesn't run in your family?" she jibed. "Daddy says sleepwalking does. He knows four kids in one family that walked in their sleep, and one time they all got up at three o'clock in the morning and made sandwiches and sat around eating them and drinking Kool-Aid. I'll bet you Poco can't top that for queer."

"No," Savannah agreed, "that tops anything Poco ever did." She hoped this was true. "How does your father know so much about sleepwalkers?" she asked.

"He's a pediatrician, Savvy! Pediatricians treat kids for more than just chicken pox, you know. Listen, do you want to sleep over again tonight? Aurora said I could invite you."

"Okay. I'll go ask Bessie and come right back. Okay?"

How easily she spoke of *Bessie* now. How like a ditdot she sounded, with her casual okays sprinkled in! Maybe she came off cooler than she felt. Well, so *okay.* Savannah admired the McWilliamses. They accepted her, they didn't mock "hoigh toiders" the way some dingbatters did; and Savannah knew she could ask any one of them for help, if she ever needed it.

Already she felt better about Poco, knowing she could go to Dr. McWilliams, if that was what it took to get him cured. Dr. McWilliams was a pediatrician. He was used to treating kids for sleepwalking; Mary Jean said so herself.

7

◆ A Creative Piece of Work

Ms. Paisley took the whole week of the Headquarters fire to mark their compositions. *Beautiful!* she wrote on Savannah's. *A +*.

After school on Monday, still mellow from her teacher's praise, Savannah reread her composition during the ferry ride.

A VISIT TO MY ROOM

My room has a secret staircase. I told my best friend about it, but I wouldn't tell her where it was. Just looking, no one would ever guess. There are twin beds in my room. My best friend sleeps in the one by the wall, when her mother lets her sleep over. My friend looked under both of the beds, but even she knew that is a dumb place to look for a secret staircase.

On the wall beside the closet there is a built-in bookcase where I keep my books and my games and my record collection. My friend likes to look through my records and I let her play her favorites on my stereo. In front of the bookcase there is a round table with two chairs where we play Cootie and Boggle. We eat lunch there, when my mother lets me invite her. My friend thought she would find the secret staircase behind the bookcase, but she didn't.

On one side of the door there is a chest of drawers and on the other side there is a vanity dresser. I keep my collection of T-shirts in the chest of drawers. I have twenty-three T-shirts in my collection, all from different places in North Carolina, except for one that my parents brought me from a convention in Hawaii.

My friend looked and looked for the secret staircase. She finally gave up and I told her to stick her head out the window. Guess what she saw? There is a wooden fire escape outside my window that was put there a long time ago before our town got the water tower. My friend said it was a good joke when I told her that was the secret staircase!

"I want you all to listen to a creative composition," Ms. Paisley had told English class, and she had read the paper aloud in the extravagant manner Savannah adored.

"Shoo! Twenty-three!" somebody in the back of the room exclaimed, when Ms. Paisley read the part about the T-shirts, but Savannah didn't care. Kinky Fulcher was the only Breacher in her classroom, and Kinky had never been inside the Guthrie house, much less Savannah's "room."

During lunch period, Ms. Paisley took Savannah aside. "Do you enjoy writing, Savannah?" she asked. "Your paper shows a lot of talent." Savannah squirmed. "Um, that room I wrote about isn't, um— maybe I kind of exaggerated about it, how it is in real life."

The teacher lifted her arms dramatically. "But it was a marvelous composition! I *want* you to be as creative as possible in my class." Ms. Paisley, new to teaching this year, wore her enthusiams with as much flair as she wore her trendy clothes.

Savannah relaxed. Creative. Grammaw would have called it lying, but what did Grammaw know? She still drew water from a cistern.

When she had assigned the paper, Ms. Paisley had written four topics on the blackboard to choose from:

A VISIT TO MY TOWN
A VISIT TO MY SCHOOL
A VISIT TO MY HOME
A VISIT TO MY ROOM

Initially, Savannah had considered writing about middle school, which she and seventh grade Breachers attended on the mainland for the first time this year, the town having dropped the junior high system. In previous years, students had not gone upland for their education until they entered high school.

For his composition Kinky Fulcher had written a rambling, ungrammatical paragraph about the town of Breach Island. That had been Savannah's second choice, up until that first Saturday morning at Mary Jean's inspired her to appropriate her new friend's room.

"Showen owf, that's what you done," Kinky Fulcher accused her on the boat ride home after school. A lurch of the ferry thrust his leering face into hers. "You got nothen loike a room what old Pissley read out today."

He snatched the paper from Savannah's hands. "*A +* ?" he shrieked. "Oi don't believe it! Pissley gave you *A +* for wroiting thet peckoloys?"

Savannah retrieved her paper. "*I* did not *write* a *pack* of *lies,*" she denied, enunciating.

"'Ayee didd nott wr-r-rite'" Kinky mimicked. "Listen at you, towken loike a ditdot, troyen to towk loike old Pissley."

Savannah turned her back on him, to savor her pleasure. If even Kinky noticed, maybe she really did sound like Ms. Paisley. She slid the English paper into her notebook and prepared to leave the ferry.

Kinky crowded up beside her at the bow. "Where's the far scape on you'erns house? I never seen no far scape."

"It's been torn down."

"Your folks never gone to Hawaii, neither. I a good mind to tell old Pissley on you."

For a brief space Savannah weighed the risk of saying to Kinky, so what? Ms. Paisley doesn't care what I write. She thinks I'm creative.

But Kinky had no real interest in the fire escape or Hawaii. "Is that yellerhead ditdot really your best friend?" he inquired. His fleshy lower lip hung slack while he awaited her answer.

Savannah looked past him at the dour brown pelican standing sentry on a piling beside the ferry slip.

"Her, you know, the one that you come into the C.Q. with," Kinky insisted. He positioned himself within the line of her vision.

Savannah turned her head to survey the drawbridge upstream from the ferry slip. Two men in orange vests hammered at the structure's near leaf. The bridge had been meant to connect Breach Island with the mainland for over a year now but they kept having trouble with the mechanism that raised metal flaps on the roadway and allowed masted boats to sail through. A regular school bus was supposed to loop around Breach and pick up the island's kids, if they ever got the bridge to working right. Savannah hoped that never happened. She preferred using the ancient three-car ferry that now pocketed itself neatly into its slip.

Kinky grabbed her arm. "That yellerhead gives me kind of a fish-eye ever time you'erns come in at

Creamy Q. She say anything to you about me?"

"Not much." Savannah shook off his hand. She unlatched the pedestrian gate and trotted down the gangway.

"Not much?" Kinky swung along beside her. "That means she said *something*. Tell me what she said about me."

"You don't want to know."

"Yes I do." Kinky turned confidential. "Listen, Savannah, that lil yellerhead is one ditdot I don't mind the looks of. You could tell her that, I wuun't mind. Tell her she can drop anchor at my buoy any time she wants to, tell her."

"That would surely give her one big thrill," Savannah drawled in Ms. Paisley's voice.

"You think so? Honest?" Kinky capered in delight. His booted feet crunched the shell roadway. He snapped his fingers. "You know what, you're all right, Savannah. Being you'erns is best friends, you could fix it up between me and her, if you'd a mind to."

"Oh, I'd like to do that, Kinky, I really would. I already know Mary Jean is interested in you."

"Sure nuff? She tell you so?"

"Well—not in just those words, but she did ask me about you."

Kinky's pale eyes glittered with greed. "Wha'd she want to know?"

"I better not say. She might not like for me to."

"Come on, Savannah! I won't tattle on you. Just

tell me what it was she said!"

"Well, all right then. Mary Jean said—" Savannah paused.

"Said what? Said what?" Kinky implored.

"She said, *What makes that weirdo talk so funny?*"

Kinky fell back. His rubbery mouth worked foolishly to cushion his hurt. "Lying jackass!" he screamed, retreating. He kicked a furious spray of crushed shell against her leg. "Everybody knows what a liar you are!"

Creative, Savannah corrected him in her mind; but in her heart she regretted her spiteful jab. She had gained nothing for herself in uttering a deliberate cruelty. Furthermore, she could be sure, knowing Kinky, that he would find some way of getting even. It was just a question of time.

A sour taste rose and trembled in her mouth as she continued on her way to Grammaw's house. What would Kinky do to get even? And when?

8

⚎ Grammaw Stoves the Ditdots

Kinky Fulcher was actually a distant cousin of Savannah's on her mother's side. Grammaw could tell you in detail how everybody on Breach Island was somehow related to everybody else, either by birth or marriage; but regardless of what Grammaw said, Savannah wasn't about to admit kinship to a beast like Kinky.

When she was only a third grader, she had watched him capture a fuzzy mongrel puppy that had wandered onto the school playground at recess and while the puppy wiggled in his arms and licked at his face, had seen Kinky deftly light a match and set afire the animal's fur. From the window of his office, the principal had seen too, and had rushed out to the puppy's rescue.

Savannah sat at Grammaw's table and tried not to remember how the frenzied puppy tore about the schoolyard with a flame riding its back. Why couldn't she forget those hideous screams of pain, that agonized somersaulting? And the horror did not fade with time. Even now she fancied she could *smell* the putrid stink of singed fur. Inside her head she heard Kinky's cheers as the puppy eluded its pursuers.

Between them, the principal and the playground monitor managed to corner the crazed animal. The principal tumbled it over and over in the grass to extinguish the blaze. "Take it in to first aid and see about doctoring it," he ordered the monitor. "I'll handle this one." He collared Kinky just as the bell rang ending recess.

The blows of the paddle resounded in the third grade classroom, as they resounded now in Savannah's memory, and made her cringe. What if some day she should be the one singled out for the public humiliation of a paddling?

Oh, don't be so sensitive, Mama always told her; they're not going to whip anybody that behaves herself. But school paddlings, when they occurred, still shocked Savannah, and obscurely shamed her.

Most of the students, however, took satisfaction in Kinky's bellows that day, for few in the school claimed him as a friend. He was older and larger than the other kids in third grade, having repeated for two years running, and he bullied his classmates whenever he thought he could get away with it. Kinky's mainsail, Savannah's Grammaw declared, didn't go all the way to the top.

Savannah fingered the bread on her plate. Nearly

every day after school she stopped in for a snack at her grandmother's weather-beaten cottage. Piecing out the day's grub, was how Grammaw described the little meal they shared along with the day's gossip. Savannah stirred her tea. "Kinky Fulcher called me a liar today," she said, scrounging comfort. (She saw Kinky's blubber mouth working; once more she heard the blows of the paddle.)

Grammaw said, "All the Fulchers got a plucky tongue, Savvy. Kinky come honest by hins."

A chubby cast-iron stove with the name *Evenheat* embossed across its belly stood at the hub of Grammaw's living room. Year round Grammaw kept it stoved, in her words, for all her cooking and heating. Beside the front door and handy to the cistern outside, a tarnished metal dry sink clung to the wall. A flowered cretonne frill concealed its wastepipe and some crude shelves nailed in below the sink.

This old house nourished Savannah as much as her grandmother's stout words did, or homemade bread. Oh, she wouldn't want to go back to anything like Grammaw's slop jar or to the lumpy rope-spring bed it stood under; but the mere presence of these homely furnishings calmed certain tides within her that she had not yet identified.

"Looky here, I want to show you something." Grammaw rummaged behind the cretonne frill and brought out a legal-looking document with a backing of blue paper folded over and stapled at the top. She handed the document to Savannah. "What you make of thisn?"

PETITION

We, the undersigned, residents of Breach Island, North Carolina, in our concern for the deteriorating ecology of SHACKLEFORD BANKS, and in recognition of said BANKS designation as part of the CAPE LOOKOUT NATIONAL SEASHORE, do urge and petition THE NATIONAL PARK SERVICE OF THE UNITED STATES GOVERNMENT to proceed with all due speed in the development of SHACKLEFORD BANKS, with the aim of halting, or at least slowing, the deterioration of said BANKS.

Below the typewritten message of the petition, the names of Thomas F. McWilliams, M.D. and Aurora Y. McWilliams headed a short list of signatures.

Savannah said, "Where did you get this?"

"From the ditdot woman wears her nightgown to the post office, calls herself Roar. That they bought the Evangelicals's parsonage, her and her husband. Rag round her head and strings twix her toes."

Roar. Savannah couldn't keep from laughing. Grammaw just didn't comprehend how artistic Aurora was. Mary Jean had an easel in her bedroom, but Aurora kept easels all over the house—in the living room, in the dining room, in her bedroom. She even set up an easel in the kitchen, where she dabbed and swore at her cooking and dabbed and swore at her painting until the supper started burning, or her family started hollering to eat, whichever came first. Once Savannah had seen her fling the skillet into the sink and her easel into the pantry, and before you could say Crack-me-a-crab they'd all jumped in the car and headed for the Sanitary Fish Market and Restaurant in Morehead City.

Grammaw raised her voice a scornful octave. "Says, 'Ma'am, you prolly know everybody on this island, we preciate you hope us out, ask a few folks sign they names on this here paper.' Stand there rucking up her nightgown."

Savannah said, "She's an artist, Grammaw. She designs her own clothes."

Grammaw sniffed. "Look like a nightgown to me. Says, 'You got a mighty pretty place here, Ma'am.' She figure I collect her names for her, if she fleech me a little bout my place. I give a purty to see what the inside of *her* place look like."

"Oh, it's beautiful, Grammaw! You think Mama's newfangled, you ought to see the stuff Aurora's got in *her* kitchen. The latest of everything."

Everything. If it plugged in, Aurora owned it. Mary Jean said her mother envisioned herself as a gourmet cook, and she bought all the equipment gourmet cooks used, in the belief that made her one. So far it hadn't worked, for in fact, Aurora hated cooking. Her unused appliances accumulated in perilous towers on the pantry shelves: Crock Pot, food processor, electric skillet, blender, pasta machine, waffle iron, juicer, toaster, deep fryer, mixer.

Grammaw possessed no more kitchenware than her own mother had, a few iron pots and skillets, and a well-seasoned rolling pin made of hornbeam wood. Beside her water bucket she kept a large conch shell— an ideal dipper for Grammaw, who insisted that she was "left-handeder than a conch."

Mama continually begged her to fix the place up with bottle gas and running water, but Grammaw said things worked good enough to suit her. They worked good enough to suit others as well. Evenheat turned out bread and cakes and pies that people like Aurora McWilliams fought to buy at the church bake sales.

"Says, 'Ma'am, it's for your own good, attract tourists, bring prosperity to Breach Island.' What she think, we want to live in some fool musement park?"

Savannah looked down at her plate. She liked Aurora. She liked all the McWilliamses.

"Who she git to sign? Only the ditdots, them that been coming in, buying up our property. Ain't no high tider gonna sign her paper for her."

Savannah divided her bread into diamonds, which she arranged in a lighthouse pattern on her plate.

Grammaw said, "Swayze around that jam on your bread, why don't you, hon. That's my new jam, I just put it up last month. Little some mommicky, is it? That's how come you ain't eating of?"

Grammaw spoke the language of Shakespeare, if anybody on Breach did, though she lacked the poet's fluency. She labeled as mommicky whatever she considered mixed up, messed up or merely misunderstood.

"You know it's not mommicky, Grammaw." Savannah answered sincerely. She loved Grammaw's robust sea-salt bread, and the dark, gummy jams she made from the muscadines that hedged her chicken pound. "This is your best jam ever."

"Well." The old lady grunted, pleased. "Don't you let Kinky Fulcher fidget you, Savvy. If your daddy was a pure white man, he'd brace that boy for his plucky talk, he would then." She clamped her mouth to seal this judgment on both Kinky Fulcher and Savannah's daddy's Indian blood.

Grammaw's pronouncements were usually single-minded, a natural heritage on the isolated island where she had brought up her children in accordance with her own rearing. Although Grammaw had grown genuinely fond of David Guthrie, the man her daughter Bessie had so rashly married, she could not bring herself to forgive him the fraction of Indian blood that coursed in his veins. It had been her ancestors against his for fishing rights on Shackleford, and later, for the choice building sites on the tiny scrap of poor land called Breach.

That her ancestors had prevailed amounted, in

Grammaw's view, to simple justice. Indians were
stingy, shiftless, immoral, dirty heathen: she had it on
her parents' word, who heard it from their parents
before them.

Her stringent view allowed for this slight correc-
tion, however: it seemed that the despised Indian
blood must have leached out of Savannah and her
brother, leaving them pure and perfectly white, for
Grammaw admitted to no flaw whatsoever in her
grandchildren. And woe to the wretch who did.

"Don't you pay no mind of Kinky Fulcher," Grammaw advised. "That whole Fulcher set is stuck on
theirselves."

"Kinky's stuck on Mary Jean," said Savannah. "He
told me so."

Grammaw's eyes sparkled. "Can't cut bait from a
jellyfish. Ain't she learnt that yet?"

"Mary Jean is kind of boy crazy," Savannah
granted, "but she isn't interested in Kinky. She's real
nice, Grammaw. I wish she lived here all the time, instead of just weekends. She's my best friend now."

Grammaw's back straightened. "What you saying
of? Your folks know bout you swimming with the ditdots?"

"Sure. Mama lets me eat lunch over there all the
time. And Daddy says it's okay, whenever we go get
ice cream at the C.Q."

The blue eyes widened. "Your daddy gives you
money for the Creamy Queen?"

"No. Aurora does. Mary Jean's mom. What's the matter with that?"

Grammaw snatched up the petition and folded it decisively twice. She opened the stove vent and thrust the blue square inside. A merry little blaze lighted the row of slots on the vent. "You know what's the matter of that," she said tartly. "You know very well what."

9

⚜Poco Turns High Tech

"Grammaw says before we know it, we're going to have apartment buildings and condos and shopping malls all over, and McWilliamses are to blame," Savannah told Poco.

They sat together on the school bus en route to Breach Island Elementary. They had been catching the bus ever since the first of November, when the drawbridge to the mainland had at long last begun operating. The route took them first to drop off Poco and the grade school kids before looping back and across the bridge to the middle school.

Grammaw's dire prophecy only delighted Poco. "Maybe now we'll get a mall with a video arcade," he said.

On a trip last month to Beaufort, Daddy had taken Poco along and treated him to a game of Karate Champ; and now the boy was hopelessly hooked on high tech. He spent hours in the school library, fiddling with the computer there, and more hours read-

66

ing the computer magazines the librarian let him bring home.

Computers made people obnoxious, Savannah decided. Not only did Poco speak an insufferable computer jargon, he disputed every remark she made lately.

The school bus edged past a truck hauling a mobile home. Another *Wide Load*. Savannah sighed. Already three kids from the new trailer park on Breach had started riding the school bus. "Grammaw says Dr. McWilliams went right to the top of the highway department. That's why they finally got the stupid bridge to working."

Poco said, "It's not stupid. I can get to the video arcade easier now. There's always somebody driving over to Beaufort. I ruthered the ferry burnt up, like the excursion boat did, ruther than cars waiting in line all morning before they get on."

He ruthered the ferry burnt up. . . .

Savannah thought of the blue-tip kitchen matches. Didn't Poco hear himself, when he made frightening remarks like that? She said, "I liked the ferry. I hate the school bus."

"You just say that because your teacher told you to."

"She did not!"

"She did. The day they opened the bridge, you came home from school and told how she said it was a mistake."

"She didn't say it was a mistake, and she didn't tell me to say it." Savannah fixed him with a lofty glare as the school bus pulled up to the rear entrance of B.I.E. "In case you didn't know it, Pocosin, I am capable of formulating my own opinions."

"Hah! In case you didn't know it, your opinions all sound like Ms. Paisley *formulated* them first."

"Fat," she denounced him, before he could escape. "You're a wide load, do you know that, Poco? You're so fat, you look like Kinky Fulcher." That wiped him. She could see the hurt mottling his face as the bus pulled away.

She didn't care. If Poco talked ugly to her, she had every right to talk ugly back. Ms. Paisley did *not* say the bridge had been a mistake. She merely said that even a slight change affected the ecology of an island; *for example,* she said, the bridge over to Breach.

Savannah stared morosely out the window. Poco used to be sweet, she brooded. What was happening to her brother? If ever anybody needed a cure, Poco did.

The realization came to her, nagging her, that she hadn't seen any fires on Shackleford since the Headquarters disaster. The talk had died down, too, just as Grammaw had predicted. About time for the next thing to happen, the next blaze to flare up, to make them take notice—which Grammaw had also predicted.

What next? It could be anything. It could happen

any time. Somebody with a chip on their shoulder could set fire to the old ferryboat, say, now sitting idly in its slip. Poco would see it burnt, he said, before he'd go back to their old, slow way of getting across the river, three cars at a time. *He ruthered it would burn,* Poco said. . . .

On the upper loop of the island, the bus paused to pick up Kinky Fulcher. He flopped in the seat ahead of Savannah but immediately turned around to taunt her. "Look what the net hauled in that the suckers won't eat."

"Must be talking about yourself," she retorted.

The minute Kinky boarded, the whole bus started smelling of fish. Lately he had been helping his father weigh in the catch before school in the morning. Big bucks, he bragged.

Moreover, the elder Fulcher allowed Kinky to drive the company pickup now, around the docks, and to the post office and back. Kinky was not eligible yet for a license, but Kincaid Fulcher declared that his son driving the pickup was every bit as legal as some underage farm kid driving a tractor. The tractor was "an implement of husbandry," North Carolina law said, and a fourteen year old could operate one on his own property. In any case, Breach Island's sole police officer was a Fulcher.

Since the bridge had opened, Kinky confided to Savannah, he had made a lightning trip to Beaufort that neither his father nor his uncle, the police officer, knew about. "Vr-r-rooom! That little pickup of mine has got *scat*," he boasted. "Twenty minutes flat, door to door. Couldn't do that, a-course, without the bridge be fixed."

Which reminded him: "I hear tell the ditdots over by you'erns was the ones got our bridge fixed. Must be big in Raleigh, for that."

Savannah said nothing.

"Prolly what makes the gal so stuck-up. The yellerhead gal. What-cha-ma-caller."

"Mary Jean," Savannah said between her teeth. "Her name is Mary Jean. And she isn't stuck-up, not the least little bit."

"Natchally you wouldn't call her stuck-up: she the one that allus pays for the cones, when you'erns come to the Creamy Q."

She opened her mouth, stung, but she couldn't think of a comeback. Kinky spoke the truth and they both knew it.

Savannah never had money to spend—and she didn't want any. Daddy needed it worse than she did, if he was ever to save enough to build the marina he dreamed of owning. It wasn't his fault that outsiders kept coming in and buying property and driving land prices up to where he never stood a chance, right there on his own island.

Kinky said, "Me, I wouldn't want no ditdots paying for me."

Savannah said with dignity, "Mary Jean is my

friend. When she pays for the ice cream, it's because it's her turn. We take time abouts—her one time and me the next."

"Huh! I don't see *you* buying no cones."

"That's because my mother makes good desserts. Mary Jean's mother doesn't, so when we eat over there, we have to go get ice cream instead."

The part about Mary Jean's mother was true enough. The rest was creative, sort of. Mary Jean had never actually come to lunch at the Guthries', but Savannah had been intending to invite her for a long, long time now.

"As a matter of fact, it's my turn," she said. "I already asked her over, their next trip down, and her mother said she could come. In between Thanksgiving and Christmas, Mary Jean told me. After we have lunch at my house, I'll treat her to dessert at the Creamy Queen. You just wait. I'll show you who buys the cones."

"Go ahead, show me," Kinky sneered. "Back Sound'll freeze over the day you pay."

*

Ms. Paisley projected a vegetation map of Shackleford onto the screen in front of the class. A little more than one hundred years ago, she said, maritime forest covered the long, narrow sand bar, making it altogether habitable—which indeed it was, for the settlers there who earned their living by whaling and fishing off its shores.

"But their livestock foraged," she said, "and the settlers cut trees to build houses and boats, and they cleared the pocosins for gardens, until today, as we know, the island is barren, except for this tiny forested area"—with a pointer she circled the landward tip of the island—"here in the westernmost quarter."

Guthrie's Knob, Savannah noted with satisfaction. Her Indian ancestors had not despoiled Shackleford.

Ms. Paisley shook her head. Alas, the forest's survival could not be credited to the Indians' stewardship, she said, with a regretful smile for Savannah. Guthrie's Knob had merely been smaller than Diamond City, with less potential for abuse.

"And do you know where Diamond City is today?" She struck the Atlantic Ocean with her pointer. "Here! Under the water! One structure alone can profoundly alter an island's ecology," she reminded her class.

For example, the Breach Island bridge. If the ferry ever burned, they'd be stuck with the bridge forever. And across that bridge the F.B.I. man would speed, to jail the one who burned the ferry.

Savannah found a ragged fingernail to gnaw. How long did you have to stay in jail, if you burnt a ferry?

10

🔸 What Bridges Are For

"I hate the new bridge," Savannah told Ms. Paisley, in the cafeteria line at lunchtime.

The teacher raised a quizzical eyebrow. "Why, Savannah, surely you're not opposed to progress."

Savannah took her tray to a vacant corner table to puzzle that one through. Was Ms. Paisley for the bridge, or was she against?

"Understand, I'm neither for nor against the Breach Island bridge," said the teacher, as though responding to her confusion. She unloaded her tray on Savannah's table and sat down across from her pupil.

Savannah decided to take a stand. "Well, I'm against it," she announced. "I liked riding the ferry. With the bridge, pretty soon our island will have apartments and condos and shopping malls all over it. With video arcades."

"I think you have to accept that some people enjoy those things, even though you don't. Change brings advantages along with the disadvantages, you know."

"My grandmother doesn't think so. My grandmother says she doesn't need anything modern."

Ms. Paisley smiled. "I doubt that even your grandmother would be willing to give up her TV."

"She doesn't have a TV," Savannah said. "No TV and no radio. She doesn't have a bathroom, either. She gets her water from a cistern."

But even as she spoke, Savannah recognized that Grammaw wasn't as backward as she made her sound: she did have electricity. Savannah could remember when, and almost why, Grammaw had stopped using candles. She still didn't own a fridge, or any other electrical appliance, but she took remarkable pride in the single naked bulb that swung from the center rafter in her house.

"Cut on my lectric, young'ern," she'd say. "Now, don't that make a purty light?" Oh, Grammaw wasn't as self-sufficient as she pretended.

Nor was Savannah immune to progress. "I guess I am just as glad we've got a bathroom at our house," she confessed.

Ms. Paisley nodded. "There always seem to be trade-offs to any change," she said. "You may not like what the bridge brings onto your island, but the same bridge also takes you *off* the island. To school, for instance. And a girl like you is definitely going to plan on college, for another instance. Then, after that—wherever you choose to go in life. That's what bridges are for."

Savannah thought, College? College cost money. Wouldn't she be lucky just to graduate from high school? Neither Mama nor Daddy had gone off Breach Island for education. The ferry would have taken them to high school in Carteret County, even back then, but Daddy's folks said it was time he started earning his keep, and Mama's thought high school was frivolous, especially for girls. Grammaw had not gone to school at all.

"Let's divide this piece of cake," said Ms. Paisley. "It's more than big enough for two."

*

That night Savannah sat up late, applying herself to her homework as Ms. Paisley said good scholarship candidates did. When she finally went to bed, her mind was still spinning from all the lunchtime talk of community college and financial assistance, so she was ill-prepared for her first good look at the night-walker.

She thought she had not yet fallen asleep when, aware of some movement in the room, she sat up and observed a spectral figure rocking from side to side, as though in grief, at the foot of her bed. It was one of those white nights, white not from the moon but from the ghostly luminescence of water mirroring the clouds over Back Sound; and in its light she could see the nightwalker plainly.

She knew at once that she beheld Poco's spirit, al-though she could not see its face—in fact, took care

not to see. The old Corees forbade gazing upon the
face of a nightwalker. This apparition was the very
image of Poco. Hefty, she observed. Ponderous in its
movements. And not at all scary, nothing like the hor-
rifying figure she had glimpsed briefly in the skiff that
night.

Far from feeling afraid, she longed to console this
spirit—if spirit it was—for she understood by the
melancholy waving of its arms, the languid gesturing
of seaweed under water, that it yearned for wholeness, sought wholeness.

She watched it drift from the foot of her bed to the
door and back, and along the walls. It was a funny
little nightwalker; it wore Poco's pajamas, and seemed
devoid of substance in the way it floated about, oblivious of obstructions in the room. It appeared to drift
right through the wooden table that held Mr. Coffee
and the TV set. Its movements mesmerized her; she
felt light-headed and turned her gaze aside. When she
looked again, the nightwalker had vanished.

She sat for awhile, wondering. Why hadn't she spo-
ken? Why hadn't she offered help? She lay back
down, wondering. *Was* that the nightwalker, or was
it really just Poco, sleepwalking again? Had the vision
been a dream? She felt mildly confused by the whole
episode. Presently she fell into an uneasy slumber.

*The front door clicked, and Poco entered the house.
He had gone looking for the nightwalker. She wanted
to ask if he had found it; wanted to tell him that she
had seen it here earlier, in this very room; but Poco*

walked past her to the table. He was fully dressed, he wore his weather boots and lumber jacket. "Fire," he mentioned, almost to himself.

And indeed, looking out, she saw two fires on Shackleford, twin torches, shaped and reshaped by the wind.

Poco ran his hands over the surface of the table until he found what he was looking for, the computer magazine he had left there. He opened it to the right place and slowly, methodically removed two pages. He handed Savannah one. She did not have to question him. When he rolled up one corner of his paper, she followed suit; together they spindled their pages into identical tapered cones. Poco twisted the tip of his. Savannah crimped hers. Together they approached the stove.

Poco pulled a match from his pocket and lighted the front burner for them. "Go," he instructed. Simultaneously they touched the two paper tips to the blue fire. Each flared up hotly before settling to the uniform flame it had been fashioned for. Their slender torches would burn in tandem right down to the last bit of paper that remained in their fingers; they would light every candle in the house. It was all in the spindling of the paper; they had done their job right, the way Grammaw had taught them.

They watched their candlelighters being consumed. They watched one another. Savannah could see fire eating close to Poco's fingertips. *Drop fire!* she begged him silently; *please drop fire!* He set his mouth and

made no outcry. The putrid smell of searing flesh sick-
ened her. She caught her breath and slapped their two
flames to extinction. "You win," she said.

He stared at her wide-eyed, blank-eyed.

She stared back, breathing hard. There must be a
way to make sense out of all this. She asked, to break
the silence, "You want to go to the bathroom, Poke?"

He did not answer. Instead, he clomped onto the
porch and, climbing into bed, covered himself completely, from boots to cap.

"Oh, Poco," she whispered tremulously. This sleepwalking business was crazy. It was getting so bad she
was scared to go to sleep, for fear of some new weird
stunt she might get involved in. The very next time
the McWilliamses came down, she promised herself,
she was going to talk to Mary Jean's daddy. Dr.
McWilliams was a pediatrician. He ought to know
why a perfectly normal kid like Poco walked in his
sleep, and what she could do to make him stop.

"Are you all right, Savannah?" Her father entered
the house so quietly that she had not heard him. He
laid an arm across her shoulders.

With an effort, she controlled her voice. "I'm all
right, but I'm not sure Poco is."

Daddy said, "What do you think is wrong, honey?"

"He's out on the porch in his bed, all covered up
with his clothes on."

"Maybe he got cold and put on another layer to get
warm."

"His boots too?" Daddy's easy unconcern irritated

Savannah. "Poco got dressed to go *outdoors,* Daddy. He put on his weather boots and a lumber jacket and a boggan. Like he was going somewhere. Like he expected to be out in the cold for a long time. Now take a look at those fires, over on Shackleford."

"Are you saying Poco set them?" Daddy stroked her arm. "Poco's too little for such as that, Savvy. Figure it out for yourself. It's too far over there for a little guy to row, and set a fire, and row back. You ought to know by now he was only sleepwalking. Try not to worry about it. He's back in bed and safe, that's what counts."

"That's all that counts? You're just going to let him sleep like that? In his boots and jacket?"

"No, of course not. He would worry about it in the morning. I'll change him into his pajamas before I go up. Don't you think it's time now for you to get some sleep, too?" He urged her toward her sofa bed.

She huddled under the quilt, dissatisfied, still irritated. Daddy kept saying Poco was "too little" to blame. He wasn't too little. He was almost as big as Kinky Fulcher.

And how come Daddy always showed up whenever Poco got into some scrape? When Daddy fished at night, he didn't usually haul in till morning. What time was it now, anyway?

*

Mama said, at breakfast, "What's this mess all over my clean floor?"

Poco said, "How would I know? What kind of mess does it look like?"

Ashes, Savannah thought, with a surge of dismay. They forgot to sweep up the ashes.

Mama stooped down and looked close. "Like somebody'd been burning paper." She put her hands on her hips. "You and Savannah haven't been playing that awful game again, have you?"

Savannah made a gesture meant to look impatient, but she held her breath until Poco answered.

"What awful game?" Poco's blue eyes were all innocence. "I don't know what you're talking about."

11

✤ One Last Look at Shackleford

Savannah knew exactly what game Mama was talking about, but she wasn't about to admit she and Poco had been playing it. How old was she the last time— seven years? eight? That meant Poco must have been only about four, so perhaps he honestly didn't remember any game, when he said he didn't know what Mama was talking about.

But he obviously remembered how to roll candle-lighters. Back before Grammaw got her electric, she kept on the dry sink a squat ironstone jug decorated with a gray-and-tan picture of a grim Queen Victoria clutching an orb and scepter. Grammaw had inherited the jug and she kept it filled with candlelighters. She had practiced this small economy lifelong to save matches, as had her Shackleford ancestors: a single candlelighter would light every candle in the house. It had been Savannah's job, and Poco's, to keep the jug stocked.

They tore pages from an old Sears catalog and

spent whole evenings rolling candlelighters. Poco liked to finish off his with a twist at the tip. Savannah swore by crimping. Grammaw stoved the ones she said they had rolled slunchways. She demanded quality workmanship and they strove to give her what she wanted.

Young as he was, Poco could roll a mighty snug candlelighter; he had to: in the game, his work competed with Savannah's. They only got to play when Grammaw was out of the house, so it was important.

The game worked like this. The minute Grammaw stepped outside, to pull collards, say, or to coax a broody hen from the nest, Savannah and Poco would fly to the jug and select their candlelighters, hers a crimped one, his twisted. They took their mark at Evenheat's slotted vent, they made ready with their weapons. When Savannah said "Go!" they thrust their tapers through the vent openings until the paper tips ignited, then carefully withdrew them and manipulated their flames to make them last as long as possible.

They were both good at the game, and they were fairly evenly matched. They constantly worked to improve their time, for the real object was to see which player chickened out first and had to drop fire, in dread of burned fingers.

The game measured bluff as much as bravery, and Savannah invariably won. And Poco invariably cried—not much, and not very loud, of course; but as the fire crept closer to his fingertips, he would start tuning up.

"Don't cry, now," Savannah would caution him.

"I'm not," he always quavered.

"Because Grammaw will want to know why, if you cry, and she won't let us play any more."

"I'm not crying," he would insist, his voice breaking into a wail—but a muted wail—just before he dropped fire. He would still be whimpering as they set to work afterward, scuffing the telltale ashes to powder on the sanded floor.

The threat of pain panicked him; Savannah could see that; but he was a little trouper, Poco was. He wanted to blubber, but instead his face would work mightily, he would squeeze his eyes shut tight and bite his lips; and by the time Grammaw came back into the house, he would have controlled all except the rage he couldn't quite conceal.

"Storm a-comen on," Grammaw would say, observing his expression. "Whattamatter, hon?"

"*Nothing,*" Poco would snarl.

"Face looks like the night *Chrissie Wright* come shore." The horrendous wreck of the *Chrissie Wright* on Shackleford, long before Grammaw's time, actually, still lingered as a Breach Island measurement of foul weather, nasty temper, or just plain bad luck. "What did you do to him?" she would ask Savannah.

"I didn't do anything to him. We were playing a game and I won, that's all."

"Well, now, I wouldn't get mad over a little thing like losing a game, if I's you," Grammaw would tell Poco. But she would pet him up and jolly him some and ask him if he wouldn't like to help her fix some fried cornbread to eat with molasses; and later on she would take Savannah aside and mutter, "Why don't you let him win, hon, oncet in a while?"

The time came when Poco gritted his teeth and hung on until he blistered his fingertips, and for all his resolve, lost anyway. That time he couldn't stop himself from crying. He bawled and bawled.

Grammaw brought a leaf of her burn plant in from the garden and squeezed its gel onto his blisters, but that didn't shut him up. She bathed his face and held him on her lap and promised him boiled custard and still he bawled.

And of course Grammaw found out about the game, so that was the last of that. That was the last of her candles, too. She locked them up in her hurricane chest and dumped the contents of the Victoria jug into Evenheat. Then she went downtown and ordered her electric which, from the day they strung it overhead, she adored. One yank of the chain and presto! Light! She said her electric cost maybe a wadjit more than candles but it was worth it.

Savannah smiled to remember the tantrums Poco used to pull, back when he was little and they played the candlelighter game. He wasn't nearly so emotional now. Last night, in fact, he had behaved mechanically, almost like a robot. . . .

"Fire," Poco had said, in a robot's electronic voice.

Savannah's scalp prickled. She wondered if the nightwalker ever talked, wondered if its voice sounded like a robot's—wondered, in fact, whose voice she had been hearing, whose face she had been looking upon last night. Those vacant eyes, that didn't look like Poco's, his ponderous way of moving, what if—what if—?

She shook her head dazedly and tried to think of something else, not to descend too deeply into the What Ifs.

*

Daddy rowed over and spent the night before Thanksgiving at Guthrie's Knob so he could get up early and shoot duck for their holiday dinner. A lot of islanders had switched to turkey in recent years, but Daddy said he meant the Guthries to stick with tradition as long as they had a tradition to stick with. After New Year's, the feds probably wouldn't allow shooting on the Banks. They had already outlawed the killing of loons. His kids had never even tasted stewed loon.

Savannah said, as he was preparing to leave, "Take me with you, Daddy. Please!" She hankered for one last look at Shackleford, before it changed forever.

She could tell it pleased Daddy, that she wanted to go with him. He said, "Well, babe, if you'd like to—"

Mama said, "There's nothing but garbage to see, Savannah. You don't really want to go over there."

"Yes I do," said Savannah.

"You said it was boring when we went in the summer. And now it's cold weather to boot."

"It's not cold today. It's nice out."

"Let it blow up a good sheep storm and you won't think it's nice. The shack is drafty, and it's just plain dangerous at Thanksgiving time, with them shooting off guns at everything that moves."

Daddy winked. "Aha." He knew Mama hated guns and shooting. But he said, "Your mother's right, Savvy. Let's wait till the weekend. We'll pack our lunch and all of us go over for the day. You can get enough of Shackleford on a picnic, without freezing overnight in a fish camp."

Bad weather intervened that weekend, however, and good fishing preempted the next, but one Friday morning in mid-December, Daddy came in jubilant from a big mullet run and said, "How about today, folks? Gonna be a nice one."

Mama got right up from the breakfast table and started making their sandwiches. As it happened, middle school had adjourned on Thursday for a teachers' workday, so the picnic fitted in perfectly for Savannah. Poco couldn't go, though, because his school had already used up its workday.

Crossing the sound in the skiff, with the sun hot on her back and the oarlocks grating, quawk-quawk, Savannah mused about Great-Grandpa Guthrie, who had floated the homeplace from Guthrie's Knob to its new location on Breach Island. The champion oarsman of Shackleford, driven off the island by a rogue hurricane. How unfair it seemed that a hundred years later his descendant was to be driven once again from Guthrie's Knob. Quawk-quawk. Overhead a heron, the one they called a quawk, echoed the wail of oar-locks.

Gradually the blur of Shackleford came into focus. A shining blade of sand bar knifed the horizon. Its handle at the landward end, where the maritime forest grew, raised a green knob against the limpid western sky.

An uplander wouldn't believe you, if you told about weather like this in the middle of December, balmy, without a breath of wind and the water dead slick calm.

They were close enough now to scan the empty stretch of sand flats toward the lighthouse. Not a fisherman in sight. It looked as though they'd have the Banks to themselves. On a nice summer day, Daddy reminded them, the ditdots would be standing butt to butt, fishing from those flats. In the wintertime, the real fishermen got their island back.

Beneath its bland deceptive surface, Back Sound washed over treacherous shoals. When the waves troughed deeply, novices often clapped bottom. You could easily go aground, even if you knew the channels. Daddy told his favorite story about Old Pa Willis taking a ditdot to Shackleford for the day.

"'Where are all those shoals I hear so much about?'

says the ditdot; words scarce outen his mouth before Old Pa sets onto a sand bar.

"'Well, this is one of them,' says Old Pa, slick's a greased eel. The ditdot never knew but what Old Pa set onto the shoal to oblige him."

Daddy maneuvered a deft course skirting Middle Marsh. Savannah filled her lungs with the wonderful, pungent aroma of salt marsh at low tide. She loved that odor. Slimysmell, Mary Jean called it.

Daddy eased the skiff into Shackleford Slue. "Going home," he said. Nearly always he said that when they went to Shackleford Banks.

Today Savannah heard the nostalgia in his voice and she repeated his words with emotion. "Going home."

12

⚑ Going Home

Daddy said the Guthries had always called Shackleford home. His great-grandpa, Westard Guthrie, settled on Breach after the big storm, but he missed the primitive life of the Banks. Most of the folks on Breach did. Before too long Westard built the Guthries a fish camp down on the Banks, near the remains of Diamond City, so his people would always have a place on Shackleford to go home to.

The bad blow of '99 seemed to spawn even more storms that eroded the beach and forced moving the fish camp farther and farther westward on the Banks—that was how they started calling Grandpa Westard. The camp, in Daddy's time, passed to an uncle's branch of the family, and Daddy, after his marriage, built his own camp right where the original homeplace had stood.

Guthrie's Knob occupied the slight elevation that counted for a hill, at that end of Shackleford. Atop it, Daddy's one-eyed shack surveyed Back Sound from a thicket of live oaks and red cedar, above a narrow sand wall bounded by freshwater marsh.

You entered the shack through a low door at its rear. Across from the door, the structure's single eye, a curved automobile windshield, looked out to where a finger of bare sand clawed its way up from the wall and into the thicket. Daddy had paid a dollar for the windshield, salvaged from a skeleton Oldsmobile set upon cinder blocks in Kincaid Fulcher's front yard. A web of hairline cracks on the driver's side radiated from a silvery point where a pebble had starred the glass.

"Home sweet home," said Daddy. His hut had sheltered him through many a blow.

"A home only a man would build," said Mama, with a scuff at the dirt floor.

Daddy defended his handiwork. "They don't make shipwrecks the way they used to."

Before radar, nobody had to bring in lumber. At almost any season a man could build from a score of wrecked hulls along the beach. No longer. For his shack, Daddy had pieced together siding of warped plywood and battered panels from aluminum dinghies. Stenciled across a scrap of Fiberglas that must have been some boat's transom Savannah made out the faded letters CHRIS RY—

Another *Chrissie Wright* came shore, she thought to herself.

Its furnishings were as sorry as the shack itself. A

pile of salt marsh hay for Daddy to sleep on. A tattered tarpaulin, stiff with resin. A rusty metal container, rectangular in shape, and a rusty metal container, cylindrical. The hut contained no fireplace, no stove; Daddy opened cans and ate from them, when he stayed overnight here, and he brought up a battery lantern from the boat, for light.

They went outside and followed a narrow trail around Daddy's trash heap into the thicket. Beyond a stand of yaupon hollies, dwarfed and carved by salt spray, the path plunged into a dense growth of stunted trees and shrubs wound round with vines. Here grew close clumps of shrubby marsh elder, wax myrtle, and bamboo vine.

Savannah broke off a sprig of holly. "Don't you even light a campfire sometimes, Daddy? You've got yaupon here; you could boil water and make tea. I'd fix me a grill out of that big old tin can and cook me a flounder on it."

Daddy shook his head. "Too risky. A little wind, a spark flying into the pocosin, and poof! Some of this stuff burns like butane." Berries scraped from the myrtle oozed wax at the pressure of his fingers. "Your Grammaw's people made their candles from these," he said.

The tangle of thicket stopped them. Savannah, stooping and hunting for the path, could see stitches of white sand threading past a bowed and strangled juniper. Animals beat trails all over Shackleford,

Daddy said. The path had been tunneled into the pocosin by wild goats, descendants of those abandoned here after the hurricane exodus.

You couldn't get close to any of the island's livestock, you saw cattle only at a distance, ranging by themselves or in small groups. On Shackleford, indeed everywhere on the Outer Banks, a layer of fresh water floated on salt just beneath the surface of the sand bar. Wild ponies pawed for it wherever thirst took them. The herds had grown too large and were destroying the vegetation. Next year, when the feds took over, they would round them up and remove them from the Banks.

Mama said, "Is anybody getting hungry?"

"We can eat right here," said Daddy. "Indoors or out?"

"Out," said Savannah.

Mama glowered at the trash scattered around Daddy's shack. "I'm not eating in this dump."

Savannah said, "Inside, then."

"It's just as bad inside. Why don't we get in the boat and go eat at Diamond City."

"Underwater?" said Daddy.

"You know what I mean. I want to see what's been burned, down at my folks' end of the island."

So Daddy poled them back to where he could lower the engine's prop and ran them down close to Barden Inlet. Across from the lighthouse, they waded onto the desolate sand flats that separated sound from sea.

Daddy swung his arms in an arc. "It's all ours!"

Savannah pondered the ocean, today a slumbering tyrant. In the deeps beyond Diamond Shoals lay countless drowned ships from centuries past, cradling countless drowned sailors. Graveyard of the Atlantic, people called those waters.

Today a benign Atlantic rolled silkily and lathered the beach with creamy foam—a summer ocean all green and glistening, edged in lacy scallops. Low dunes pimpled a narrow strip behind the beach. The few fish camps that had not yet been leveled dotted the sand flats back of the dunes.

"My Pappaw built that one there, the one on stilts," said Mama, pointing. "See the clothesline? That's what I remember as a kid, clothes flapping on the line. My grandmother washed every day. If it wasn't clothes, it was split salt mullet, hung out to dry."

Savannah didn't remember Mama's Pappaw. His camp had long ago passed to some distant cousins.

Where the cabins had burned, they beheld the dismal wrack of charred timbers already bleached gray under the relentless eye of the sun. They saw shattered windowglass, blackened hinges here, a half-burned mattress there, among the sparse grasses of the sand flats. Trash lay everywhere. Garbage eddied in coves on the sound side.

The whole island was a dump! Savannah thought. She wanted to blame it on the day-trippers, but she had seen the same sort of debris around Daddy's camp—plastic bags and bottles and cartons, fruit rinds, rusting tin cans, discarded clothing, Styrofoam potsherds. Home, sweet home, indeed!

"Fulcher's place was here," said Daddy, counting off the casualties. "Jennings's there, Peabody's, Moss. Forty-seven of them burned down so far." His voice thickened with satisfaction.

"Who did it, do you think?" Mama asked.

Daddy's eyes narrowed. "Who's to say?"

Savannah observed his closed expression. He knows something! she thought. Daddy's keeping something secret, he's not even telling Mama! "I'm hungry," she said uneasily.

13

☘ How Mama's Folks Lived

Amid the rubble of Kincaid Fulcher's burned-out cabin a metal dinette table stood, set about with four metal chairs as primly as though prepared for company. Salt spray and sand had scoured the blistered enamel from the furniture. A blush of sand rippled across its horizontal surfaces, in a design of embryonic dunes. Daddy swept clean the table and brought their basket and water jug up from the boat. "Soup's on," he announced.

Mama said, munching her sandwich at Fulchers' table, "Well, I don't see the sense of all this burning. The Park Service would have bulldozed everything after the first of the year, when they took over, and saved some firebug the trouble."

Daddy's face tightened. "It's our island. Always has been. All of Kin Fulcher's people fished out of here; he figured he had a right to do what he wanted with his own place."

"It wasn't his land to build on, though," Mama argued. "My folks knew that twenty years ago, when the government bought up the Banks."

"Well, we all knew the feds didn't care. Nobody cared about the Outer Banks until the ditdots started hollering about saving the nation's heritage. What about *our* heritage? We were here first. It wouldn't hurt to let us keep our family camps."

Savannah looked off in the distance, to where she thought Diamond City lay. "My teacher says even one building on a beach hurts it."

Daddy grunted. "The goats are what do the damage over here, not the buildings."

"Ms. Paisley says wild ponies can't learn to protect the Banks, so people must."

"Yeah, well, your Ms. Paisley probably thinks she's some swell authority, sitting in a schoolroom and telling other folks how to run their business. If she worked the water for a living, she might talk up a different story."

Daddy spoke strongly, but later, when Mama took Savannah off to find a bathroom, she looked back and saw him glumly gathering up litter. He trailed behind him a giant's necklace of discarded plastic jugs strung together by a cord through their handles.

Savannah said to Mama, "Nobody's at your Pappaw's place. Why can't we go use his bathroom?"

"You know there's no bathrooms on Shackleford," said Mama. "One reason I never liked coming over here. The whole entire Bank's a sewer."

"Maybe they've put in a john since. Can't we go see?"

"I think you just want to snoop around. Go ahead, there's nobody to stop you. Personally, I've seen enough of fish camps to last me a lifetime."

Mama set out for a distant clump of yaupon, and Savannah approached the shuttered cottage.

Beside the clothesline stood the low parallel bars of a net spread, its gray beams scoured smooth from generations of sandy nets dragged across for drying. Savannah fondled the polished wood. At home, she and Poco still walked Daddy's net spread, sometimes. It took good balance to keep your footing on the slippery timbers.

A metal dinette table with matching chairs, like the set at Fulchers', furnished the tiny screened-in porch of the camp. The single room adjoining the porch contained a two-burner kerosene stove and an ancient dry sink. Six bare bunkbeds, in tiers of three, occupied one whole wall. The bedding had evidently been stored for the winter. The floor had been scrubbed and sanded.

Corroded aluminum screens veiled the camp's three windows, and wooden eyelid shutters on the outside further darkened the room. Savannah removed one of the screens and raised the shutter by its prop. Sunlight poured in. Against a background of purest Carolina blue, the black-and-white diamonds of the Lookout lighthouse loomed, dramatized by the window frame.

Savannah heard a tread on the porch steps and called out, "Come see the lighthouse, Mama. It looks close enough to touch."

Mama did not answer and Savannah turned around. The F.B.I. man stood in the doorway.

The shutter prop fell from Savannah's hands. Remotely, she heard the bang of the wooden blind. Her mouth tried to say "Mama!" A gigantic wave rose inside her head and her mind struggled sluggishly against its engulfing crest. "I thought you were Mama," she finally managed.

He wore the same clothing she had seen him wearing on the ferry, but his pants were baggy now and his boots dingy. He did not look at all surprised to see her. "Is this your folks' place, young lady?" he inquired.

"No, ours is Guthries'—" Savannah stopped herself. Her hands shook and she hid them behind her back.

"Guthries. Lots of Guthries in these parts. Which one is your daddy?" He studied the room as though searching for Daddy.

Savannah said, frightened, "There's more of the Yeomans than there are of us." She took a breath. "More Gaskills, too. Midgetts, Fulchers—"

The man walked over to the two-burner stove and scratched around in the match holder nailed to the wall alongside.

Maybe the man did not remember her! Savannah

sidled toward the door. "Robinson, Wahab, Rose," she babbled. "Those are all big families around here. Jennings, O'Neal." She tried feverishly to think who else. "Willis," she squeaked.

The man knelt and peeped underneath the dry sink. Savannah bolted.

"Wait a minute, kid," she heard the man call after her, "let me ask you something."

Savannah flew down the steps and across the sand flats to Mama, returning form the clump of greenery. "Oh, Mama!" she panted. "Mama! That man came in the house while I was there."

Mama seized her arm. "What man?" she demanded. "What happened? Are you all right, Savvy?"

"Sure, I'm all right. Nothing happened. It was the F.B.I. man, the one that was on the ferry asking about the Headquarters fire. Don't worry, I didn't tell him anything."

When she heard the man had merely poked around in the fish camp, Mama loosened her grip and gave a sardonic sniff. "Still thinks he'll learn something, snooping around, I guess." She allowed Savannah to steer her back toward Daddy. "I don't know what you'd tell the F.B.I., anyway. You've done nothing wrong."

Another skiff floated next to theirs, where Daddy had anchored. Daddy said, "Fellow claims he come over to do a little fishing, and asks me for a hook! Some smart fisherman."

Savannah said, "That wasn't any fisherman, that was the F.B.I. man, Daddy!"

Daddy started loading his necklace of plastic bottles into the boat. "You don't say."

"The one I told you about, on the ferry that morning, remember?"

Daddy grunted.

"Did he tell you he was from the F.B.I.? Did you know who he was?"

After a long silence, Daddy said, "He didn't tell me anything, but I knew. Everybody knows."

Mama said, "Did you give him a hook?"

"I got none to spare for his kind. Hooks nor anything else."

Daddy had plenty of hooks, Savannah knew. He never went out in the skiff, or any boat, without his tackle box. "I'm ready to go home now," she said uneasily.

Mama said, "I knew you'd get your fill, before the day was out."

In the skiff going home Mama talked about the big oyster roasts they used to have, on the Banks. Clambakes, said Mama. Stewed drum with flour dodgers laid around the sides of the pot.

She remembered the one large dune she and her sisters played on, Buzzard's Hill, and swimming afterward, to wash off the sand, and families cooking their dinner outdoors together. "There's nothing tastier than salt mullet with the roe, cooked over a wood fire, after a day in the open," Mama said.

"I thought you'd seen enough of fish camps to last you," Savannah reminded her.

"I have. When I think of how my folks lived—well, I'll take my comforts, any old day. And clannish? It's a mercy your Grammaw didn't marry me off to my cousin Royal, when school let out. Land, she don't turn me a-loose till yet. Aproned out and wearing a bonnet I'd be, same as her, wasn't I married and with a house of my own."

Savannah said, "Grammaw doesn't even like me to wear blue jeans."

"Well, I'm all for progress," said Mama. She preened her elaborate hairdo with satisfaction.

Savannah saw the McWilliamses' gray Buick turn into the parsonage driveway just as Daddy tied up to their stake. Mary Jean hung out the backseat window waving madly. Savannah hit the landing on a run to meet her, before she remembered and turned back to Mama. "Can I ask Mary Jean over for lunch tomorrow?"

"I think it's about time you did," said Mama. "You've eaten off of them every weekend since school started."

"Can I take her to the C.Q. for ice cream afterward? That's what we always do when she invites me."

"Ask your father. He's the banker."

Daddy's face darkened, but he said, "Okay, babe. Remind me in the morning and I'll give you the money."

And Grammaw talked about him being stingy!

Savannah tore up the path yelling "Mary Jean! Mary Jean!" She couldn't wait to see Kinky Fulcher's face when they walked into the Creamy Queen tomorrow.

14

✵ Kinky's Offer

But she didn't rush right up and lay it on Mary Jean that afternoon. She intended for the invitation to sound casual, like Mary Jean's invitations. Cool.

So, on Saturday, "You want to stay for lunch?" she asked, very cool, out on the porch where they were reading old *Dennis the Menace* comics aloud to each other. She hollered to Mama who stood out in the yard hosing salt film off the windows, "Bessie! Is it okay if Mary Jean stays for lunch?"

Mama shut off the water and stood there puzzled, perhaps at hearing herself called Bessie, but more likely because Savannah had spent half the morning picking out crab for the salad and fixing the table nice for company. "Sure," Mama said at last. "Happy to have you join us for lunch, Mary Jean."

"If you want to," said Savannah, very off-handed.

Mary Jean looked doubtful. "What's for lunch?"

Mama tightened her mouth a little bit. "Nothing poison."

A tiny throb of apprehension began to pulse in Savannah's stomach.

At the table, Poco wiggled during the blessing. "Oboy, crab roll!" he burst out, when Daddy said Amen. He snatched a bun and grabbed the bowl of crab salad.

"Wait a minute, son," said Daddy, "Company first."

Poco paused in puzzlement. "Who else is coming?"

"Nobody *else* is coming—she's already here. Mary Jean is Savannah's company."

Poco's ruddy face turned ruddier. He got along great with Mary Jean; people he got along great with weren't company! However, he recovered handsomely. "Take all you want," he said to Mary Jean, yielding the bowl.

She said with distaste, "What's this? Fish?" But even Mary Jean must have thought how that sounded, for she added, "You must be like my Mom and Dad. They're big on fish."

Mama said, in the pleasantest voice imaginable, "Folks that catch fish for a living eat fish every day."

"Here, take one of these." Poco slapped a bun onto Mary Jean's plate. "You want two? I always eat two. I might get three if you don't take seconds."

"No danger!" Mary Jean giggled. She deposited a sample smear of salad on her plate.

"That's not the way! Didn't you ever eat a crab roll? Here, let me show you." Poco grabbed the serving spoon and ladled up a gob. "You put it on your bun, like this, and then you put on your top, like this, then you kind of smoosh it all together—"

"Whoa, there!" she squealed. Filling oozed from all sides of the bun.

Savannah said, "Don't give her so much, Poco."

"Aw, that's not much. Watch how I fix mine, Mary Jean. Crab roll's best if you got potato chips. You put chips on top of the crab, before you smoosh it down, and when you taste that, man, you're eating rare. Mn, mn! You got any potato chips, Mama?"

"Not today, Pocosin," said Mama.

Poco said, "Go ahead, try a bite." He bit hugely. "Ayfe," he urged Mary Jean.

"What?"

"Ayfe! Ayfe!"

"Make him stop, Mama!" Savannah pleaded.

Mary Jean shouted, "I can't tell what he's saying!"

Poco reached in with a finger and moved the mouthful to one side. "Taste," he pronounced thickly.

Mary Jean screamed with laughter and pounded on the table. Mama and Daddy exchanged a level glance.

"That's enough of that, boy," Daddy ordered.

Mama said, "Pocosin. Don't talk with your mouth full."

Poco strained and swallowed. "I was just telling her to taste and see how good it is."

Mary Jean nibbled at the bun. "It's not bad, for fish," she conceded.

Mama and Daddy exchanged another glance.

Savannah could not even taste her own crab roll. She chewed mechanically and tried to appear unconcerned.

"You want any more?" Poco asked, when the meal was nearly finished. At Mary Jean's refusal, he swabbed the bowl with the last remaining bun. "What's for dessert?" he demanded, still chewing.

"Rhubarb grunt," said Mama. Her lips barely moved.

Savannah said, "But Mary Jean and I aren't having any. We're going to the Creamy Queen for dessert."

"You don't know what you're missing," Poco told Mary Jean. "I bet you never ate rhubarb grunt either, did you? With evaporated milk poured over?"

Mary Jean pretended to collapse. "No, and furthermore—"

"Mayweplease be excused from the table?" Savannah telegraphed Mama a desperate plea. She knew Mary Jean had offended her parents. Daddy's face looked like dead low tide: all the underneath muck exposed.

Mama nodded permission and Savannah hustled Mary Jean out the door. Never again, she vowed, stalking off to the Creamy Queen. Daddy was right—Mary Jean really wasn't their kind. But what was Savannah supposed to do—just dump a friend if your folks didn't like her?

"That was fun," said Mary Jean, chuckling.

"Yeah. Some fun," Savannah muttered.

Mary Jean stuck a finger in her mouth and held down her tongue. "Ayfe! Ayfe!" she commanded.

Savannah managed a weak grin. Could this *Chrissie Wright* possibly be salvaged?

"'You put it on your bun, like this.'" Mary Jean heaved an imaginary shovelful of crab salad.

Savannah began to revive. "'Then you kind of moosh it all together.'"

Mary Jean cracked up. She stood in the roadway and stamped her feet and hollered. "'You want any more?' he says," she gasped. "He says, 'What's for dessert, Ma?'"

Savannah egged her on. "Rhubarb grunt, honey, yum yum yum."

"Evaporated milk poured over!" Mary Jean clutched her stomach. "Bleah, bleah!"

Savannah relaxed a little. The disastrous luncheon party might even be judged a success! And the pleasure of stepping up to the counter and paying Kinky Fulcher for their cones had yet to come.

But when Savannah actually handed over the money, she and Mary Jean had got to laughing so hard that Kinky just goggled at them and rang up the sale the way he would anybody else's.

She didn't have to prove anything to Kinky, Savannah decided. Nor did she need to defend Mary Jean as a guest at the Guthries' table. Mary Jean had to answer for herself.

They sat down in the back booth to eat their ice

cream. Her appetite had returned, Savannah realized.

Across the room Kinky Fulcher picked his teeth and issued loud instructions to Euel Jennings, whom he was training to work the counter. From time to time he glanced toward where the girls sat. When he finally caught Savannah's eye, he winked broadly and made a lewd gesture. Savannah sputtered in disgust.

"Just say it, don't spray it," Mary Jean advised her. They cracked up again.

Kinky, drawn by their high spirits, strolled back to their booth. He smelled powerfully of fish as usual. "You'erns onto goferide?" he inquired.

Mary Jean ducked her head to smother her giggles. "What did he *say*?" she muttered to Savannah.

Savannah translated. "He wants to know if we'd like to go for a ride."

"With Euel, a-course," said Kinky. "Us four."

Mary Jean looked with interest at Euel Jennings, self-consciously sponging the counter. Euel was pretty cute; Savannah thought so herself, and she wasn't even boy crazy. But she was shocked to hear her friend ask, as though she might actually take Kinky up on his offer, "Go for a ride where?"

"Oh, around. Beaufort?"

"What's in Beaufort for us to do?"

Kinky had not thought that far. He pondered for a moment, stumped. Presently he announced, "They got a Creamy Queen in Beaufort, we could go get cones."

"Don't you guys have to work?"

"After work, I mean. We close up four clock, winter."

"How would we get there? You're not old enough to drive."

"Yes I am. I drive for my old man, all time," Kinky boasted. "I'm the one got the wheels, see?" He indicated the pickup parked out in front. Kincaid Fulcher, Fish Dealer.

"What wheels? I don't see any car."

"There, setten right there. That there's my pickup."

Mary Jean confronted Savannah with an amused question in her eyes. Savannah shrugged. Mary Jean could do as she pleased. She, Savannah, didn't intend to go anywhere with Kinky Fulcher. Not anywhere, anytime. Period.

Mary Jean thought of a more important question. She jerked her head at Euel Jennings. "Why doesn't he ask me himself?"

"It ain't his pickup, to ask. Sides, it's me asking you, not him. Euel's stuck on Savannah."

Euel, stuck on . . . ! Involuntarily Savannah turned toward the boy behind the counter. Their eyes caught. Both looked away at once, but not before something unexpected and charming, like a shared understanding, passed between them.

"*You* asking me! In a *truck?*" Mary Jean's tone peaked with outrage. "You've got to be kidding. What kind of a hick do you take me for?"

The shock of her words staggered Kinky. He caught his breath and flung up a hand, as though to ward off a blow. "Oh, you bitch!" he sneered. "Don't you think you're purty, now!"

Mary Jean slid out of the booth. "At least I don't stink like dead fish," she said. "Come on, Savannah. Let's get out of here." She stamped to the front and shoved open the heavy glass door.

"You'll be sorry!" Kinky yelled after her. "You'll get your pay for that!"

Savannah scurried past him. She didn't care how Kinky felt, she reminded herself. But other people who weren't acquainted with Mary Jean might very well take offense at her blunt way of talking. Savannah couldn't help wondering what Euel Jennings thought of her friend.

15

❧ Fishing For Old Times' Sake

Mary Jean said, outside, "That poor guy is nuts. Did he really think I'd go for a ride with *him?*" She wobbled her head and made an idiot's face. "Cuckoo."

Savannah had her own reasons for doubting Kinky's mentality, but his infatuation with Mary Jean wasn't one of them. She said, "I'd be careful how I talked to him, if I were you."

Her friend said, "Yeah, a kook like him, you wouldn't put much of anything past him. It wouldn't surprise me if he was the one that set the Headquarters fire."

Once again, as she had the first day she met Mary Jean, Savannah found herself defending Kinky Fulcher. "He couldn't have," she said. "Whoever burnt down Headquarters did it while Kinky and the men at Fulcher's were icing the trawlers that night. They worked straight through till one o'clock. The excursion boat was already burning at midnight."

Mary Jean looked disappointed. "Well, anyway,

that fire was set by somebody about Kinky's caliber. They know where it started, and from what I hear, they must be getting pretty close to finding out who did it."

Savannah stopped walking. "What do you mean?"

"The fire. Where it started. They say it was like some kid's fire, with paper and kindling and a few wooden matches that didn't get entirely burned up. A pro would've used gasoline, they say."

"Who's *they?*" Savannah could barely make her voice work.

"The F.B.I."

"The . . . ?"

"F.B.I. You know—the man on the ferry you told about, that talked to all the kids. He came around and talked to us, too."

Savannah said, "Talked to you. . . . Didn't you think he was awful? What a phony! I wouldn't trust him with his hands tied."

Mary Jean said, "Really, Savvy? I thought he was kind of neat. He was telling Dad and Aurora last night about the lab where he worked before they transfered him to the field. He knows his stuff."

"He said a kid started the fire?"

"No no no; he didn't say a kid. But a fire somebody *like* a kid would build, or maybe somebody like Kinky, who's not very bright."

It was amazing how much the man knew about matches, Mary Jean said. How many different kinds there were and how they could be traced, even after they'd been burned up. Book matches were easier to trace than kitchen matches, for obvious reasons.

Savannah thought of the blue-tip matches in their metal safety holder beside Mama's stove. But Poco wasn't the only one in the world who could get hold of blue-tip matches. They came from Wade's store. Probably most of the families on Breach used blue-tip kitchen matches that came from Wade's store.

The McWilliamses' gray Buick turned in at the parsonage as the girls approached. Mary Jean said, "Hey, Aurora's back. She promised she'd take me to get my ears pierced, if she got home early enough. You want to come and get yours done too?"

Savannah said, "I don't have the money."

"It's free, at the Jewel Box in Beaufort. They've got this sign, 'Ear piercing done free with purchase of earrings. No extra charge for pain.' Har har har!"

Savannah laughed with her, but her heart wasn't in it. She had spotted Dr. McWilliams out at the end of his long pier. If ever she needed to talk to him about Poco, the time was now. "I'll wait and see if you survive surgery," she said. "Right now, I think I'll go see what your dad is catching."

*

Dr. McWilliams sat dangling a piece of bacon on a string.

Savannah came up behind him. "It's a lot easier if you put out crab pots," she told him. "You want me to go get you a couple of ours?"

"Thanks," he said, "but I'm fishing less for crabs

than I am for old times' sake. This is how we kids went crabbing, when I was a boy. I grew up on the Outer Banks," he explained, "in Ocracoke."

"Ocracoke! You're a Banker? But I thought—"

"—thought I was a ditdot?" he finished for her. "No, I guess I'd be on Ocracoke instead of Breach, if it wasn't so hard to get there. But doctors like me can't live on remote islands and do the kind of doctoring they want to."

That made sense. There couldn't be all that many children for a pediatrician to doctor, on the Outer Banks. Savannah hesitated. She had seized this opportunity to talk to Dr. McWilliams and now she couldn't think how to begin.

Dr. McWilliams said, "I've got enough string and bacon for us both, if you'd like to join me."

Grammaw used to take her crabbing like this, Savannah remembered, only Grammaw used a raw chicken wing for bait. She sat silently beside Dr. McWilliams, her line twitching in the indolent slap of water below.

Dr. McWilliams said, "Old Man Crab wants that bacon, and he grabs it and hangs on, but when you haul him up halfway, he looks around and says to himself, I can't breathe, I can't breathe! Give me water! and he drops off. I feel that way in Raleigh, sometimes. I need this water to get me through another week in the city."

Savannah wished she could think how to start.

Dr. McWilliams said, "Is something troubling you, Savannah?"

"Oh no . . . well, yes. It's my brother."

"What's the matter with your brother?"

Savannah said, "He walks in his sleep a lot, and I'm scared maybe he's going to hurt himself someday. Or hurt somebody else." Poco went outdoors sometimes, she told the doctor, and if you tried to talk to him, he acted crazy, and his eyes looked like he didn't hear you. . . .

"He really *can't* hear you. He's not conscious," said the doctor, "and it's better not to talk to him; that sometimes alarms sleepwalkers." Poco should be let alone at such times, he said. He would go back to bed of his own accord, and in the morning, probably wouldn't recall what he'd done.

Savannah told him, "Daddy put the latch up high on the screen door, but it didn't keep Poco inside."

"Your father's got the right idea, though. He should be aware too that Poco can hurt himself inside the house as well as out."

"That's what I'm scared of! Last week Poco turned on the stove in his sleep and started burning a piece of paper. Stood there and held it in his hand and let it burn down. He wasn't trying to set fire to anything, just watching the paper burn. But what if something did catch on fire? Accidentally, I mean?"

The doctor nodded gravely. "It could happen. Sleepwalkers aren't rational about what they do.

That's why sleepwalking should be taken seriously. Fortunately, most children outgrow the tendency and turn out perfectly normal."

"I don't think the Indians outgrew it," Savannah told Dr. McWilliams. "Daddy says they looked all the time for their spirit. When they walked in their sleep, I mean. They thought their spirit was like somebody real. They called it—him—the nightwalker, and they were scared to look at his face." She stole an uneasy glance at the doctor. She tittered. "I guess that's just Indian superstition, isn't it?"

Dr. McWilliams did not smile. "Who am I to deny their beliefs? We know so little about the mind, or the spirit—whatever we call it. With no better answers than we have, I think you have to respect the Indians' search for the nightwalker."

There. She had it on doctor's orders. Practically the same thing Daddy had said. Trudging home deep in thought, Savannah wondered why she had not been trying all along to get Poco together with his nightwalker. Her dread of seeing the nightwalker's face figured in it somewhere, she knew. But she would simply have to deal with that when the time came. She would think of something. The important thing was to get Poco straightened out before the F.B.I. caught up with him.

16

☘ Some Unexpected Fireworks

For Christmas, Grammaw gave Savannah an apron with tatted lace on the hem and three dollar bills in the pocket. Poco presented her with a bag of butterscotch drops individually wrapped in orange cellophane. The package that really surprised her came from Mama and Daddy. It contained a beautiful little teen bra with a slight but confident curve of shaping.

"What's that you got?" Poco asked, looking over her shoulder.

Savannah hid the garment in its tissue. "New underwear," she said. "Thank you, Mama. Thank you, Daddy."

"You're welcome," Mama said with a maternal smile. "I'd been thinking you were ready."

Daddy said, "I guess our baby girl is growing up."

Fortunately, they left it at that, and the day moved on to its traditional celebration. They went to church. They ate their Christmas goose at Grammaw's, as usual, and picked at the carcass for supper.

That night, after everybody had gone to bed, Savannah tried on the new bra. It fit sweetly. In the bathroom she looked at herself sidewise in the mirror. She wondered how cheap you could buy earrings and still get your ears pierced free at the Jewel Box. Mary Jean had called the moment of puncture Excruciating!, but she also admitted that she wasn't very big on pain. Savannah meant to find out exactly how excruciating, the next time her friend came to Breach.

But that wouldn't happen for months now. After their mid-December visit, the McWilliamses had closed up for the winter. The family would not return to the parsonage until Easter.

On New Year's Eve, Savannah promised to wake Poco up at midnight, to hear the firecrackers go off; but lying in bed waiting and listening for the first sounds of celebration, the hours passed slowly, and she kept dozing off. What finally happened drove all thoughts of the New Year from her mind.

Something out there. She roused and heard the distant jingle of a chain, or of breaking glass, and groaned. Poco at it again. Even from her bed she could see the fire on Shackleford, far to the west, tonight, in the area of Guthrie's Knob. And of course she didn't find Poco in his bed. He wasn't in the bathroom, either; she couldn't find him anywhere in the house.

She stepped to the door to scan the crystalline dark outside. After a long look she spotted movement next door. A shadowy figure that had to be Poco swooped back and forth under the deformed loblollies that marked the frontage of the parsonage lawn.

But was that Poco or was it somebody else? The strange ritual dance dipped and swirled in eerie circles. Savannah had seen that same effortless gliding before. The nightwalker again! Its peculiar languid gesturing meant something, and now Savannah knew what that something was—a summoning; the spirit reaching out for Poco. The chance she had been waiting for had arrived at last.

"Nightwalker! Nightwalker!" she called to the figure, but for some reason her voice worked so poorly that she could not hope to make herself heard. She hastened inside for her slippers and at the same time yanked the quilt from her bed to wrap around herself against the bitter December night. Soundlessly she crossed the porch to let herself out the door.

The nightwalker was nowhere in sight, but as soon as she pushed through the hedge, she saw the stocky form galumphing across the McWilliamses' clipped lawn, toward the house. Now it carried a large bundle across its shoulder. Wait! she tried to call out, but even as she watched, the figure seemed to dissolve in the shadow of the house.

She hurried toward the parsonage with one intent, to detain the nightwalker. If she could only persuade it to come together with her brother, she honestly believed that would end his sleepwalking. And if her guess was right, she would also bring a halt to these senseless burnings.

For a wonder, she felt no fear in approaching the figure. She had seen the nightwalker before and knew it to be harmless, a funny little thing; she had no reason to fear her own brother's spirit.

The lawn stubble caught at her corduroy slippers. She picked her way toward the McWilliamses' back door, where the nightwalker had vanished.

A measured thumping stopped her. She detected motion along the moonlit side of the parsonage, saw what caused the thumping. High above her head, Poco, in jacket and boots, climbed the wooden steps that led to Mary Jean's room. At the top he turned and stared down at her. He swung one leg over the windowsill, and beckoned her to follow. In another moment he had disappeared into Mary Jean's room.

She forgot about looking for the nightwalker. She hurried after Poco. It wouldn't be the first time she had mounted this fire escape—the famous secret staircase! She and Mary Jean often used it as their private entrance.

The shutters to Mary Jean's window stood ajar. The wintry wind fluttered curtains on either side of the shattered windowpane. Poco waited for her just inside. He took her hand and helped her step across the low windowsill. He indicated the twin bed that was to be hers, the one next the window. He drew down the flounced spread on the other for himself.

Then he crawled under the covers and lay down.

Mary Jean had left her room in a mess, Savannah saw. Her easel lay in splinters on the floor, atop a pile of crumpled paper from her watercolor block. Wads of construction paper littered the carpet. Pine cones had been scattered everywhere. Mary Jean's luxurious room looked just plain trashy.

In fact, none of this was right. Poco had no business taking over the bed Savannah usually slept in, here at Mary Jean's.

She punched his shoulder, but he did not move. Only when she pulled the knitted toboggan from his head and tweaked his ear did he seem to comprehend. He rose then and turned back the coverlet of the other bed. Instead of lying down in it, however, he clomped to the window, climbed out, and with heavy tread descended the fire escape.

Just like that! Without a word of explanation, without bothering to close the window after himself! And without turning a hand to smooth either of the beds he had rumpled.

Wasn't that just like Poco? Let Savannah do it. There was no reason *why* she should tidy up, no reason *why* she should close up after him, except that she was the sister. He probably thought that was what sisters were for. And now he had walked out on her, gone back home, leaving the mess to her. She slung Poco's cap onto a bedpost and swiftly, efficiently, remade the twin beds.

Frigid wind billowed the curtains. Cold in here. Savannah retrieved the woolen cap and dragged it down over her ears. She cloaked herself in her quilt and shivered, staring at the window. Why did she feel so dreadfully abandoned? What exactly was she doing here? She tugged at the quilt, struggled to think, to remember, What...? Who...?, tugged and tugged—

And gazed about her in dismay. What *was* she doing here, in her pajamas, alone, in the middle of the night, in Mary Jean's room? She scarcely had to ask herself the question; the answer unfolded chillingly in her mind: *she,* not Poco, was the sleepwalker.

But Poco did walk in his sleep! she argued with herself. She knew it for a fact. Hadn't she followed him around, many a night? Hadn't she followed him *here,* this very night? She snatched Poco's cap from her head, as evidence of proof. The real proof drummed inside her head: Sleepwalking ran in families. Both she and Poco were sleepwalkers.

"Must run in the family!" She could almost hear Mary Jean accusing her again, kidding her and laughing about it. Mary Jean wouldn't think it was so laughable when she saw how Poco had wrecked her room.

Savannah felt distressed and somehow responsible for the shambles. She also felt mortified by an insidious notion that came to her. For she didn't have to confess the vandalism to anybody. Poco wouldn't remember; she could slip back home and into her bed, and nobody would suspect either of them of this spooky little caper.

"You rotten sneak!" she accused herself, and then she paused, astonished by an unexpected insight. Could this deceitful, dark side of her nature be *her* nightwalker showing itself? The idea panicked her. She made for the window, but yelped with pain when a needle of glass stabbed through her cloth slipper. She stood on one foot to remove it. She massaged a trace of blood from her toe, not much of a wound, but somehow more than she could bear. She whimpered.

In the peculiar state of her sleepwalking, the shattered window hadn't even registered on her as something out of the ordinary. Just as the trash all over the floor hadn't fully registered. She took a good look around. She felt confused, spacy, still unable to separate the scary reality of *being* here from the singlemindedness of her sleepwalking, only moments before.

The strengthening light in the shadowy room added to her confusion. She grew slowly aware of a crackle from below, and a flickering of the light. She ran out to the stairway.

Fire! The hall danced with flames; flame tongues licked at the stair railing; flame fangs chewed at the stair runner; the house was being devoured.

Below, in the dining room doorway, she beheld a familiar stocky figure on hands and knees, fanning a brisk little bonfire of newspaper and pine cones.

17

The Firetrap

Savannah flew down the stairs. "Kinky Fulcher!" she screamed, and began to beat at the bonfire with her quilt.

The boy scrabbled to his feet and turned upon her a shocked countenance. He shot off into the kitchen. Savannah raced after him. She heard a crash, a rumble of falling objects, a bellow of distress.

Instantly she knew what had happened: instead of escaping out the back door, Kinky had plunged into the pantry.

Before he had time to correct his mistake, Savannah slammed the pantry door and locked him inside.

"Open this door, you!" Kinky rattled the doorknob.

Savannah couldn't help sniggering. She too had mistaken the pantry door for the back door, not long after her introduction to this household. It was a natural error, for the two doors, twins, stood side by side.

124

Within the closet, she knew, a hodgepodge of kitchen appliances, pots and pans, canned goods, and cleaning gear had been stacked precariously right up to the ceiling. The gourmet Aurora denied herself nothing in the way of kitchen equipment, except the organization of it. In dislodging a single piece, Kinky Fulcher had brought down upon himself an avalanche that doubtless had been waiting for weeks to happen.

"You hear me, Savannah? You lemme out of here, else I bust you one!"

Savannah paid no heed to his threat. She had to think of putting out that fire. She ran into the hall and swung her quilt in great frantic arcs. Flames surrounded her.

She beat and beat, following a fiery path from the dining room, along the hall and up the stairs. She could tell she was gaining on it, but many a patch she thought she had extinguished blazed up a second time, and a third. Thick smoke filled the hallway. She beat and coughed.

"What you tryen to do, kill me? I kill you, you bitch!"

"Oh, shut up!" Savannah shouted. She coughed. She swung desperately at the last persistent circle of flame on the dining room carpet. Oh, how she wanted, oh, what wouldn't she give, just to lie down, right here, and pull the quilt over her head.

She stopped beating with the quilt and started coughing in earnest. Choking, she made her way to the back door and jerked it open. Cold, clean air rushed inside. Her whole body heaved as her lungs fought for oxygen.

"You gonna catch it, girl, you gonna be sorry!" From the sound of him, Kinky had found some heavy tool, or appliance, to ram against the pantry door.

Savannah tried the kitchen lights, but none worked. That figured. Dr. McWilliams must have shut off the power at the service entrance. She groped her way into the laundry room, located the fuse box, threw the main switch.

A bare bulb above the fuse box blazed, assaulting her eyes. Squinting, she ran through the downstairs. She turned on the porch lights. She turned on kitchen lights, the hall light, the dining room light, the light on the stair landing. She wanted to scream with joy and triumph. She had done it! She had conquered the fire.

And then she took a good look at the house.

Scraps of charred newspaper and half-burned pine cones lay everywhere. Greasy swirls filmed the once-white refrigerator and sink. She saw blistered paint, scorched wallpaper. An acrid petroleum odor arose from the carpet, blackened in a dozen huge circles and still smoking.

Ought to douse those places with water, Savannah thought tiredly; but the faucet when she tried it gave forth no water. Dr. McWilliams had done a thorough job of closing up the house.

She struggled to collect her wits, to try and think where the water cutoff valve might be located. Just as she started for the laundry room, to look in there for it, Kinky with one violent shove burst through the pantry door and landed sprawled on the kitchen floor.

Instinctively Savannah snatched up a large curved instrument that lay on the kitchen counter. An incongrous tool, out of place in this kitchen. She knew that tool well: a heavy iron gaff, used for hooking large fish in and out of boats. With the weapon ready in her hand, she edged around the fallen Kinky toward the door.

He leaped to his feet and headed her off. Into the galley end of the kitchen he backed her, and trapped her between the sink and the refrigerator. "Gotcha!" he snarled. His pale eyes menaced. He advanced slowly upon her.

"Touch me," she dared. She raised the hook.

He read the resolve on her face and hesitated. "Touch *you*?" He sneered. "Don't you wush. Don't you just wush."

"I definitely do *not* wish," she snapped. "You fish brain. Look at the wreck you've made of this house."

He said murderously, "You bitch, you better look I don't serve you the same." He added in a high, uncertain whine, "A stuck-up bitch, that's what you are, you and her both."

Savannah said, with sudden intuition, "Why, Kinky. You did all this because of Mary Jean, didn't you? You got mad because she made fun of you." She looked past him at the destruction and said in wonder, "You would actually burn down her house because of one stupid thing she said."

He shrieked insanely, "No I wan't. No, I ain't! What I care any fool ditdot got to say bout me? You a liar, Savannah, everbody knows what a liar you are!"

Savannah persisted. "If you didn't care what she said, then why did you do it?"

He appeared to reflect, to calm down. He actually smiled. He rocked from one foot to the other, and his pale dilated eyes turned crafty. "Maybe I didn't do it," he said, spacing his words.

"Good joke, tell me another. I *saw* you."

"You and who else seen me?"

She opened her mouth, but no sound came out.

"Look at you," he jeered. "Your hands is black, your clothes and face all dirty, that don't come from roasting marshmellows, girl. How you figure splaining what you doing this house middle the night?"

"I was putting out the fire," she spluttered. "You're the creep that has to explain."

"This creep don't have to splain nothing." He sauntered toward the back door. "All's this creep got to say is, I been home in bed ever since ten clock. *I never been in this house in my life!*"

"Oh, haven't you, then?" she shouted. "I've got this, to prove you're guilty." She showed him the iron gaff, its wooden handle branded with the name of its owner—Kincaid Fulcher, Fish Dealer.

"I'll tell em you stold it," Kinky blustered.

He could do that, she realized: her word against his, after all.

But then, blessedly, incredibly, she beheld Kinky's father, and hers, standing in the open kitchen doorway. Before she had time to wonder how much they had seen and heard, the elder Fulcher struck his son a savage blow that knocked Kinky to the floor. Bright blood spurted from his nose.

Kinky screamed. "Ow, ow, oh, don't, Pa! No! Don't hit me no more!" He writhed on the floor and scrabbled crabwise, with upflung arms shielding his head.

His father grabbed one of the arms and jerked the boy to his feet. "Git your butt up from here," he snarled. "I tend to you at home, you be begging me not to do worse'n bloody your nose!"

But his brutal words gave way to other emotions as he collared Kinky. The harsh voice broke in despair. "Git home now, young'ern, you and me better—git on home—" He hustled Kinky out the door.

In the silence that followed, Savannah turned with dread to her own father. How would he react to her part in all this? Her Daddy, too, had a hasty temper.

"Savannah!" said Daddy. She heard a tremor that sounded, to her astonishment, closer to tears than temper. "Oh, my little Savvy. Are you all right, honey?"

18

ᛞ Another View of the Nightwalker

The story blew with hurricane force across Breach Island. A *Lookout* reporter with cameras slung on both shoulders knocked on the Guthries' door while they were eating a midmorning breakfast and pleaded for an interview with the heroine of the night.

Savannah refused. She didn't want her picture in the paper. She didn't even want to talk about it, to that woman or to the *News and Observer* man who showed up ten minutes later.

"I'll talk!" Poco volunteered. "I was over to the McWilliamses before Savannah was. Can I let them take my picture, the next one that comes?"

"No, you can't," Savannah told him.

"Can I, Mom?" Poco appealed to higher authority.

"Not if Savannah doesn't want you to."

Poco jumped up from the table in a temper. "Dammittall! You'd think Savannah was the only one around here that walks in their sleep!"

Daddy said, "Watch your mouth, boy. You know better than to use that kind of language in this house."

Grammaw arrived, just about busting with the gossip from Wade's store.

It seemed that Kinky Fulcher had broken down and told how he tried to jimmy his way into the parsonage with his father's fish gaff. When some new locks on the kitchen door thwarted him, he ran up the fire escape and smashed his way into Mary Jean's room. There he wadded up sheets from her watercolor block and splintered her easel for kindling.

Grammaw told everything twice. Savannah couldn't very well shut her up. Later in the day she had to listen to more from Mama, gleaned from her church circle.

Kinky had plotted to connect a string of blazes that would flash and build quickly to a holocaust, Mama had heard. Downstairs he crumpled a trial of newspaper. He wished for a can of gasoline; it would take something volatile, he knew, to ignite his kind of firestorm.

Kinky Fulcher was a boy of rather sluggish intellect, but at this point genius struck him. Kinky thought of pine cones. When you lit a match to heaped pine cones, they practically exploded.

"Whoosh!" said Poco, repeating what he heard at school, on Monday. "That fire was a booger! Melt all the carpets, run along the hall, run up the stairs to the top of the house!"

"Oh, really?" said Savannah. "You saw it? You were there?"

Poco strutted a little. "I was there before you were."

With the resumption of school, Poco had been able to boast of his participation in the event that had eclipsed the holidays.

Savannah was getting plenty tired of listening to reruns of Kinky's misdeeds. Nobody on Breach Island wanted to talk about anything else. Even Daddy contributed a tidbit which he had picked up at the post office. Kinky, he announced, had admitted to entering the parsonage on at least one occasion before the night of the fire.

"The F.B.I. checked it out that time," Daddy said, "thinking it was someone hunting for drugs, it being a doctor's place, but they didn't find anything missing. Just some candy wrappers dropped in a few places, and soft drink containers left sitting around half empty. That's how they knew it was probably some kid that broke in."

So Kinky knew his way around inside the parsonage, even in the dark. On the first occasion, his gaff had easily pried open the kitchen door. The night of the fire, he had to break an upstairs window to get in.

Taking his gaff down to the kitchen, he had forked a huge plastic trash bag from under the sink. From inside the house, he had no need to force the kitchen door. He had only to release the chain guard, the double deadbolt, the nightlatch—and the door swung free.

Outside, loblolly cones lay in abundance on the

parsonage lawn. The resin they exuded suited Kinky's purpose—as good as gasoline! He crammed the trash bag full and plunged back into the house with his incendiary load.

From then on his scheme proceeded very much according to plan, until Savannah arrived on the scene to do battle. Her bravery had spared the McWilliamses' house.

"I wasn't brave," Savannah told her father. "I was stupid. Every time they have a fire drill at school they tell us: The First Thing You Do In Case Of Fire Is *Get Out.*"

Savannah hadn't felt like tackling school yet. Mama said she could lay out until some of the excitement died down, so for the last two blustery days she had helped Daddy mend gill nets out on the porch. "Stupid, stupid," said Savannah.

"Brave *and* stupid," Daddy qualified. "You could have been a dead hero."

Savannah allowed a wry smile. "Maybe next time I'll know better."

"I hope I've learned a lesson, too," Daddy said. "I figure I must have spooked you with those fairy tales about the nightwalker and the fires on Shackleford."

Fairy tales! Savannah meditated. Obviously Daddy had never seen the nightwalker. She thought of Poco's funny, sturdy little spirit, meandering around her sofa bed and right through the table, that night of the candlelighter game. It still seemed real to her. Furthermore, the knowledge that she had a shadowy side to her own nature bothered her.

She said only, "The fires weren't fairy tales, Daddy."

He looked troubled. "There's more than one of us that wishes we'd never commenced that mischief."

He and the other fishermen had flared their own shacks, he confessed, to protest the National Park Service taking over their traditional fishing grounds. The nightwalker story he had concocted out of his people's lore, for Savannah's benefit, to keep from revealing his part in the deed.

The high tiders meant no real harm by the Shackleford burnings, at the outset. Breachers were becoming resigned to the intrusion of government, as well as of uplanders, into their way of life. But beneath the placid surface of the community, coals of resentment smoldered; and old grievances had mounted with the Shackleford burnings until they finally erupted in the Headquarters disaster.

"Do you think Kinky burned the excursion boat?" Savannah asked.

"I don't know who did it." Furthermore, Daddy didn't want to know, didn't ever expect to find out. High tiders protected their own.

"My place was the last of the shacks to go," Daddy said, sighing. "I kept putting it off and putting it off— couldn't stand to face reality, I suppose. Kin Fulcher rode over in the skiff with me, to help me keep my fire out of the pocosin. On the way home afterward we saw the lights go on all over the parsonage, so we tied up at McWilliams's pier to check it out."

"The rest is history," said Savannah, with a wan smile.

Grammaw brought over a dish of boiled custard for Savannah—her standard remedy for sick folks. Why, she demanded, hadn't anybody told her about the brain doctor who had come all the way from Raleigh to examine Kinky?

"Psychologist, Grammaw, not brain doctor."

"Same thing. They figuring to get Kinky off by claiming he's a loony?"

Dr. McWilliams it was who, upon being notified, had brought in the psychologist. He said he didn't want to bring charges against a misguided youngster.

Savannah thought Kinky was a lot worse than misguided, but she decided against resurrecting the evil deeds of his past. There was already enough blame to go around. Mary Jean's cruel remarks. Savannah's own callous taunting of the lovesick Kinky.

"Oughted asked me," Grammaw sniffed. "I could tell em, Kinky got about the brains of a mossbunker. Kincaid Fulcher's mess of fish all come out of the same net. Half of em belong in the loony crib."

Savannah thought, Maybe the loony crib is where I belong. She felt all different, not loony exactly, but uncomfortable; let down.

*

On Thursday afternoon Savannah begged a raw chicken wing from Grammaw and took it with a piece of string out to the end of the McWilliamses' pier. She let down her line and sat for awhile straddling a piling and thumping it with her sneakers. No crab came to tug at her bait. If one did, she thought, she would simply let the crab run with it. What she really wanted was to relax and see if the crash and wash of flood tide would revive her.

Out in the sound, a candy-cane spinnaker ballooned unexpectedly from a passing sailboat. Someone in the bow waved at her and Savannah raised a tentative hand. The crab string twitched out of her fingers. She watched it waver gracefully into the depths of the water.

"Savannah! Hey, Savannah!" Mary Jean picked her way through the gull droppings that spackled the entire length of the pier.

Savannah jumped up to meet her. She asked at once, to fend off another rehashing of the Kinky story, "What are you doing out of school?"

"Daddy let me come down with him for the day, to see about getting the house cleaned up. Guess what I got for Christmas? A VCR camera!"

No need to distract Mary Jean from the Kinky story. Her new toy had clearly captured all her interest. "It's so neat, Savvy!" she exlaimed. "Wait'll you see. We can make crazy movies of each other and run them on TV. What did you get for Christmas?"

Savannah grinned. Same friend. Maybe not what Grammaw would call a journey friend, but so what? You didn't just chop out the pieces of a person that suited you, and throw away the rest, like fish bait. Already Mary Jean cheered Savannah up.

She said, "Well, I didn't get anything like a VCR camera, but it was a real nice Christmas, all the same. The usual stuff, mostly—some underwear, some candy, some Christmas money. We're very traditional, in our family."

"Ours too. Dad and Aurora gave each other a speedboat, but Dad says they may have to get their money back, depending on how much the insurance pays for fixing up the house."

Dr. McWilliams tramped out on the pier to greet Savannah. "I understand it was you who saved our house from total loss," he said. "And Mary Jean has helped me figure out a suitable reward for what you did. We're going to open a little college account at the bank for you, if you don't already have one, to express our thanks."

"Don't thank me," said Savannah. "Please. I don't want any reward. I was walking in my sleep. I didn't even know what I was doing."

Dr. McWilliams said, "I disagree. I believe you knew more about it than you imagine, Savannah. Your father tells me you went back that cold night and got your slippers and a blanket to keep you warm."

Mary Jean said, "Yeah, Savvy, you're making head-way. Maybe you'll get fully dressed, like Poco, next time you go sleepwalking."

Savannah tried to smile.

Mary Jean said, "I know what! I'll go get my new camera and make a movie of you sleepwalking. Want to?" She raced off to the house without waiting for an answer.

Savannah hunched her shoulders and looked for the sailboat. It was almost out of sight, but she could see that its crew had hauled in the candy-cane spin-naker.

At her side, Dr. McWilliams said, "Why don't you tell Mary Jean you don't want to make any jokes or movies about sleepwalking? You've been a good friend; you know how she is. So just tell her. She doesn't realize how worried you are about your sleep-walking."

"I'm not worried!" Savannah denied. After a pause, she conceded, "Well, yeah, maybe I am, but I don't mind making a movie with Mary Jean." She forced a little laugh. "It'll probably be fun. Good practice for the real thing, next time."

"I don't think there will be a next time." Dr. McWilliams looked her over thoroughly, as though confirming a clinical diagnosis. "I'm not a sleep spe-cialist, but I know enough to associate sleepwalking with growth. And you are a maturing young lady."

Involuntarily, Savannah laid a hand across her chest. Could he tell she was wearing her bra? If he asked about her period, she would die. She wouldn't be able to answer him, she would just have to die, that was all.

"As I say, I'm not a specialist," Dr. McWilliams continued, "but the fact that you're waking in the middle of your sleepwalking tells me your conscious mind is taking charge of those episodes now."

Savannah said, confounded, "My mind is?"

"Isn't it?"

"I did wake up," she admitted. "I didn't know I was taking charge."

He said, "Look at it in this way. Did you ever come out of a nightmare by telling yourself it wasn't real, it was only a dream?" When she nodded, he explained, "That was your consicous mind, taking charge."

The idea pleased her. She felt herself begin to relax.

"Of course, sleepwalking is altogether diffrent from dreaming," he said, "but they're both rooted in your nature. They're the shadow side of it, you might say."

Dr. McWilliams went back to the house soon after that, and while she was waiting for Mary Jean, Savannah leaned against a piling and gazed out toward Shackleford. What was the nightwalker, then? A dream? Poco's spirit? Something that came from a part of her nature that she didn't understand?

"My shadow side. . . ." she murmured.

*

That night, for the first time since the fire, Savannah went to bed without qualms.

Taking charge of her sleep—what a neat idea!

Always before she had thought of her sleep as separate, an event that happened *to* her, an event she could not control. It cheered her to think of her mind taking charge—of running her sleep, the way Mary Jean had run their first attempt at a crazy movie on her TV.

It wasn't going to work in just that way, Savannah knew. But she also knew about her shadow side now. Her nightwalker belonged to that darker side. She need not fear a part of her own nature, mysterious though it was. She could trust herself.

"Turn around, nightwalker," she could say. "Let me see your face. Look me in the eye."